STORIES ABOUT THE
BLACK
EXPERIENCE

ROBERT L. BRADLEY

VOLUME

THEY ALL CAME TOGETHER TO UPLIFT THE COMMUNITY

TWO

FIRST EDITION

First printing, 2001

Published by
Robert L. Bradley
P.O. Box 25768
St. Louis, Missouri 63136

ISBN 0-9702912-1-3

Library of Congress Control Number (LCCN): 00-091906

Cover illustration by Sharon Morton

DEDICATION

This book is dedicated to the memory of my enslaved African ancestors who were brought to the Americas to labor on plantations and in mines. Some of these enslaved Africans were skilled storytellers, and they brought their stories to the Americas with them. They told interesting stories about animals such as Brer Rabbit, Brer Fox, Brer Monkey, and Brer Elephant that talked and behaved like humans.

This book is also dedicated to the "brothers" that I worked with in my youth, played pick-up basketball games with, interacted with in barbershops, and rapped with at shoeshine stands. Some of these "brothers" talked plenty smack, rapped and rhymed, cracked funny jokes that would make you burst your sides laughing, and told fascinating stories about characters such as John and Shine. In my opinion, a number of these "brothers" could have become famous comedians, poets, storytellers, and short story writers if they had had someone to help them get started professionally; they were just that creative and gifted.

ACKNOWLEDGEMENTS

This book would not have become a reality without the support and kindness of others.

Special thanks to my wife Rosilyn for reading the stories in this book and giving me her frank opinion.

Deep appreciation to Gwendolyn Whiteside for taking the time to edit this book. Her kindness and generosity are appreciated so very much.

Special thanks to sisters Betty Bradley, Sennie Bradley, Bobbie Bonner, and Roxie Turner for their interest in this book.

Special thanks also to nieces Melba Bradley and Trina Bradley for their interest in this book.

Special appreciation to artist Sharon Morton for the cover illustration of this book.

CONTENTS

INTRODUCTION

Black people have been telling stories since very ancient times. Some of their stories have survived the passing of thousands of years and are still with us today.

Two famous black storytellers of ancient times were Lokman and Aesop; they were also slaves. Lokman lived before Aesop. Some people get the two confused. Both are best remembered today for their fables (stories that teach a moral lesson) and wise sayings.

Lokman has been called the "first great fabulist and wisest man of the ancient East." The Arabs say that he lived about 1100 B.C., was a coal-black Ethiopian with wooly hair, and was the son of Baura, who was a son or a grandson of a sister of Job.[1] Lokman's fables and proverbs made him very famous.

Aesop was a Greek slave who lived around 565 B.C. Greek writers described him "as being black with a flat-nose and thick lips." Aesop is best known for his fables, which have thrilled people down through the ages. These fables give advice and a moral. Some of his most famous fables are: "The Ant and the Grasshopper," "The Tortoise and the Hare," and "The Frogs Who Wanted a King." In the fable "The Tortoise and the Hare" a slow tortoise beat a fast hare in a race. The race began with the hare taking a big lead over the tortoise, but he became "so sure of victory that he took a nap, and when he awakened he saw the tortoise crossing the finish line." The lesson from this story is being steady can be more valuable than being fast. Aesop is also remembered for his wise sayings. For example, he said, "The world is like a true play of wheels, turn by turn one mounts and one descends."[2]

In addition to his fables and wise sayings, Aesop was also quick-witted. One time he and his fellow slaves went on a trip with their master to carry his baggage. When Aesop chose the heaviest load, the others laughed at him.[3] They thought he was stupid for doing such a thing. But in the end, Aesop had the last laugh, because in his sack was the food, which "grew lighter and lighter as the days went on until nothing was left."[4]

Aesop's fables and wise sayings have inspired people and influenced their thinking for many years. For example, the expression "a wolf in sheep's clothing" was coined from one of his fables. Turning to the African continent, we find that people there, same as in other places, enjoyed listening to stories. Africans listened to funny stories, moral stories, supernatural stories, and love stories, which were generally passed orally from generation to generation. This oral literature also included poetry, songs, and wise sayings. Talented persons called griots often provided the community with this oral literature.

The Africans who were transported to the Americas during the slave trade brought their stories with them. In the New World they enjoyed telling these African stories, which helped to break the monotony of slave life on the plantation. The enslaved Africans also created new stories that reflected their plantation environment. Some of the stories the enslaved Africans told were about clever animals such as Brer Rabbit, Brer Fox, and Brer Wolf.

In 1880 Joel Chandler Harris, a white man, formally introduced Negro animal stories to whites in his book "Uncle Remus: His Songs and His Sayings." Harris had learned these stories from blacks on the plantation and had retold them. In 1883 Harris published another book on black folklore, "Nights with Uncle Remus." Harris' books about Negro animal stories created much interest among whites. They also made him very famous.

Our probe into history shows that African people have been telling stories for a very long time, from ancient history to the present. It is only appropriate that the author carry on this African tradition of storytelling.

This book is comprised of four fictitious stories about the black experience in America, covering a time period from slavery to the present. The people in these stories encounter a variety of problems but thanks to their wit, courage, faith, strength, and determination they overcome them.

The Legend of Big Jim

▼▼▼

IN 1807 A NINE-YEAR-OLD MANDINGO BOY WAS KIDNAPPED BY SLAVE TRADERS from the Senegal-Gambia region of West Africa. After kidnapping him, the slave traders put him on a slave ship with other captives and transported them to Charleston, South Carolina. After arriving in Charleston, the cargo of enslaved Africans was taken to a slave market and sold. The nine-year-old Mandingo boy was purchased by a short, stocky white man named Henry Mills, a wealthy planter who owned a large cotton plantation with hundreds of slaves in the coastal lowlands near Charleston. Mills made the Mandingo boy a servant in the "Big House" and named him Jim.

While growing up on the Mills' plantation, Jim befriended an old slave known as Uncle Charlie, who was a gifted singer, storyteller, and banjo player. He taught Jim how to sing, tell stories, and play the banjo. Uncle Charlie also had knowledge of roots and herbs and he passed this knowledge on to Jim.

By 1819 Jim had grown into a handsome, twenty-one year old giant. On the Mills' plantation he was called "Big Jim." He stood 6' 7" tall, weighed 260 pounds, and was powerfully built. All the young ladies on the plantation admired Big Jim and could be heard singing his praises. Big Jim was also talented. He could play the banjo, tell stories, sing, and dance. Man, he could dance! He was such a great dancer with his nimble feet and flexible body. During dances down in the slave quarters, he and his lady would be all over that dance floor. But man, oh man, he could really tell funny stories. Woo Wee! When he told funny stories, he would have the slaves on the plantation falling out laughing and bursting their sides. The slaves on the Mills' plantation often said, "Big Jim can make you laugh if you can open your mouth."

The slaves on the plantation were not the only ones who enjoyed Big Jim's funny stories, Massa Henry, the slavemaster, also enjoyed them.

Among all the slaves on the plantation, Big Jim had the easiest job. His job was to drive Massa Henry wherever he wanted to go in the carriage. While he drove Massa Henry around the plantation in the carriage, Big Jim would tell him funny stories and Massa Henry would laugh so hard that the carriage would shake. Big Jim was Massa Henry's favorite slave, because he was so entertaining. He got special privileges that the other slaves didn't get.

The slaves on Massa Henry's big plantation were divided into three groups: the house servants, the skilled craftsmen, and the field slaves. The house servants consisted of Bessie, the cook; Elvira and Sennie the maids; Tom, the butler; and of course Big Jim, the carriage driver. Ben was a skilled craftsman, being the plantation cooper and blacksmith. There were also other skilled craftsmen on the plantation. There were hundreds of field slaves on the plantation, who worked in the fields cultivating cotton, rice, and other crops.

Massa Henry had a reputation as a good slavemaster. He made sure that all of his slaves were properly fed, clothed, and housed. But, of course, he wanted them to do their work assignments. In contrast, Travis Hill, a neighboring plantation owner, had the reputation as the cruelest slavemaster in the area. His slaves were always underfed, poorly housed, poorly clothed, overworked, and frequently punished. Not surprisingly, he was always buying slaves because they often died.

Sometimes the evil Travis Hill would tell other planters that Henry Mills was too nice to his Negroes and it wasn't a good idea to treat them like that because it would make them think that they were as good as their slavemaster and his family. He would then say, "Negroes were born to be slaves, and if God hadn't meant for them to be slaves, he wouldn't have created them."

Meanwhile, Big Jim continued to drive Massa Henry wherever he wanted to go in the carriage. He would take him to town, to neighboring plantations, and to social events. One day while they were riding around the plantation in the carriage, Big Jim told Massa Henry a story that was so funny that Massa Henry laughed until tears rolled down his cheeks. After he finished laughing, he said to Big Jim, "Big Jim, you have become very good at making people laugh. I wonder if you can make my sister Sue Ann laugh. She hasn't laughed since a great tragedy happened to her back in 1802. That year a mysterious fire destroyed her plantation. It burned down all the buildings, including her beautiful mansion, and what was even worse, it killed her husband and kids and all of her slaves, she alone escaped the fire. My sister was devastated by the great tragedy and hasn't laughed since. That was twenty years ago. Yes, my poor sister hasn't laughed in twenty years. Many clowns and comedians have tried to make her laugh, but none have succeeded. Big Jim I want you to try to make her laugh. I would love to see her laugh again because she has been depressed for such a long time. She lives down in Georgia with another sister of mine. I am going to go down there and bring her up here to my house to see if you can make her laugh. I believe you can do it, Big Jim."

Big Jim replied, "Yessah, Massa Henry, I believe I can make her laugh too. I'm going to give it my best shot."

When word leaked out that Big Jim was going to try to make Mrs. Sue Ann laugh, it stirred much excitement on the Mills' plantation. Some slaves were saying, although Big Jim was very funny, he had never tried to make a person laugh who hadn't laughed in twenty years. And they didn't believe he could do it. Other slaves were saying that Big Jim was the funniest man alive, and they believed he could make Mrs. Sue Ann laugh.

For a whole week Big Jim thought about how he was going to make Mrs. Sue Ann laugh. He had never tried to make a person laugh who hadn't laughed in twenty years. He was walking in deep waters. Suddenly it came to him how he would try to make her laugh; he would make her laugh by telling her the story "The Talking Monkey."

This was a very funny story about a monkey and an elephant that lived in the jungle. Uncle Charlie had told Big Jim this story when he was in his late teens. It had been brought over from Africa. Here is a short version of it:

The animals in the jungle had gotten along peacefully for years, but one day chaos broke loose. Different animals began to say bad things about each other and not speak to each other. Confusion and accusations were rampant. Brer Rabbit accused Brer Turtle of saying that he was stupid because he had gone to sleep during their race, and Brer Turtle accused Brer Rabbit of saying that he was slow and lazy. Sister Lion and Sister Tiger, who had been good friends for years, fell out and quit speaking to each other when Sister Lion accused Sister Tiger of flirting with her husband, Brer Lion. Sister Cheetah accused Sister Hyena of stealing her food and Sister Hyena accused Sister Cheetah of going around saying she was ugly. Other animals in the jungle were also angry with each other, making accusations against each other, and not speaking to each other. The angriest animal of all was Brer Elephant. He was very angry with Brer Monkey and accused him of back stabbing. When he caught up with him, he said, "Little Monkey, you talk too much. You are the one who has started all this mess in the jungle. Your gossip has caused best friends to break up. Furthermore, I've been hearing all the bad things that you have been saying about me. I thought you were my best friend."

Brer Monkey replied, "Brer Elephant, I am your best friend, I will stick by you to the end."

Brer Elephant said, "Little Monkey, you are no friend of mine, you keep stabbing me from behind."

Brer Monkey replied, "Brer Elephant, I will give you the shirt off of my back and if I have to, I will give my life for you."

Brer Elephant said, "Little Monkey, it doesn't matter what you say, because I'm going to get you anyway."

Brer Monkey tried his best to get on the good side of Brer Elephant, but he would have none of it. He continued to be angry, which eventually made Brer Monkey angry. They began to argue and call each other bad names. They argued and called each other bad names for three days and three nights, and as each hour passed, they came closer to a fight. Brer Monkey told Brer Elephant, "When I get through whipping your big behind all over the place, you will be too ashamed to show your face."

Brer Elephant told Brer Monkey, "When I get through whipping your little behind, you'll be sore and bruised for a long, long time."

Brer Monkey told Brer Elephant, "You're just talking stuff, but what I'm saying is no bluff."

Brer Elephant told Brer Monkey, "If you don't quit messing with me, you are going to cease to be."

Brer Monkey, sensing that Brer Elephant was about to tear him to pieces, began using psychology on him, trying to calm him down. And in the wee hours of the morning on the fourth day, Brer Monkey told Brer Elephant a nasty joke that was so funny that Brer Elephant burst out laughing, and he laughed so long and hard that he woke up all the other animals in the jungle, and they began laughing at the funny sight of Brer Elephant laughing. With all the animals laughing, peace and tranquility were restored to the jungle. And when all was said and done, Brer Monkey and Brer Elephant kissed and made up, and became best friends again.

Meanwhile, Mrs. Sue Ann, Massa Henry's sister, had arrived on the Mills' plantation and was ready for Big Jim to make her laugh. Massa Henry set the time of the big event for 7:00 p.m. on a Saturday in the entertainment room of the "Big House." That Saturday evening the entertainment room was filled with family members and guests, who all anticipated the big event. When Big Jim began telling Mrs. Sue Ann the story about "The Talking Monkey" she just sat in her chair and listened, showing no emotion. As he got on into the story, talking about how the different animals were making accusations against each other, she still continued to listen and show no signs of emotion. When Big Jim got to the part of the story about the verbal battle between Brer Monkey and Brer Elephant, her face showed that she was enjoying it. When Big Jim told her the nasty joke that Brer Monkey had told Brer Elephant and how it had caused Brer Elephant to burst into laughter, a smile came across her face. But when Big Jim told her how the funny sight of Brer Elephant laughing caused all the other animals to laugh, her smile grew wider and wider, suddenly she let loose a loud cackling laugh, like a volcano erupting, then she laughed and laughed, laughing so hard that her whole body was shaking and tears were rolling down her cheeks and she was gasping for breath. The funny sight of Mrs.

Sue Ann's uncontrollable laughter caused a big commotion to erupt in the entertainment room as relatives and guests fell out laughing at Mrs. Sue Ann. It took half an hour for the relatives and guests to regain their composure after laughing so hard.

Mrs. Sue Ann had never heard a story so funny. She wasn't anymore good the rest of the night. She didn't know that she could have so much fun.

The sight of his sister having a good laugh for the first time in twenty years brought tears of joy to Massa Henry's eyes. After Mrs. Sue Ann had finished laughing, a glow was on her face. She had released twenty years of stored up depression and frustration.

In making Mrs. Sue Ann laugh, Big Jim had succeeded while many others had failed. He was a hero to slaves on the plantation like Ben, the blacksmith, who had believed that Big Jim was going to make her laugh. Massa Henry told Big Jim how grateful he was to him for bringing laughter back into his sister's life.

Big Jim's success in making Mrs. Sue Ann laugh was quite an accomplishment. It comfirmed his great ability to make people laugh through the telling of funny stories.

Big Jim continued to make people laugh with his funny stories. The more people he made laugh the more his fame grew. Within a few years his fame had become widespread in the Charleston area. Many slave owners wanted to buy him, but Massa Henry told them he wasn't for sale.

In March of 1827 Massa Henry purchased a dozen field slaves from the slave trader, including a short, very dark-skinned slave named Abraham. The likes of Abraham had never been seen on the Mills' plantation before. Abraham talked plenty smack, liked a good laugh, and was very rebellious. He would tell the other slaves, "I'm tired of working for nothing; I want to get paid for my labor." Abraham always tried to avoid work. He would tell the overseer that he was too sick to work. He would say, "Mr. Jack, I'm sick; I don't feel like working in the cottonfield today." Abraham would also tell the other slaves that he was going to escape up North to the "Promised Land" where he could be free.

For some reason Abraham took a liking to Big Jim and had a deep respect for him. It maybe because he was such a great storyteller. Big Jim would come down to the slave quarters to visit his girlfriend, and on the way back to the "Big House" he would stop and talk to Abraham. While talking to Abraham, Big Jim would tell him funny stories and jokes, and Abraham would fall out laughing.

One day while Abraham and Big Jim talked, Abraham said, "Big Jim, I'm tired of being a slave; I want my freedom. I'm thinking about escaping up North to the 'Promised Land.'"

Big Jim somewhat startled, said, "Abraham, you are kidding. Running away is dangerous and risky. Suppose you get caught. If you do, you will be in big trouble."

Abraham said, "Big Jim, you have to take a risk if you ever want to be free. And I'm willing to take that risk. I'm serious about running away. Will you run away with me, Big Jim?"

Big Jim answered, "No way, Abraham, will I try to escape up North. I am not a field slave; I'm a house slave. I have it made on this plantation. All I have to do is drive Massa Henry around in the carriage and entertain him with my funny stories."

Abraham said, "Big Jim, I know running away may sound crazy to you, but keep thinking about it."

From then on every time Abraham saw Big Jim he would ask him to escape up North with him, but Big Jim would always tell him no.

On a warm day in early March of 1829, Big Jim and Abraham were talking when Big Jim asked Abraham, "Why are you so rebellious?"

Abraham answered, "Big Jim, I have this rebellious spirit because I am an Ashanti, a people known for their rebellious spirit. They love their freedom; they run away and rebel against slavery. The Ashanti and the Fula, another African people, come from an area of West Africa that the white man calls the Gold Coast. The Ashanti and the Fula are also called by the name Coromantees. The Coromantees have frequently been the leaders of slave revolts in Jamaica. I was born in Jamaica."

Big Jim said, "I understand now, Abraham, why you are so rebellious. You are very rebellious because you are an Ashanti. So, you were born in Jamaica, huh? Where is Jamaica?"

Abraham answered, "Big Jim, the island of Jamaica is in the ocean, south of us. I was born there on the Richard Bowers' plantation. I was a house servant on the Bowers' plantation until I was twenty-seven, then Massa Richard fell out of favor with me and sold me to a rich Frenchman named Pierre Cartier. Soon after Massa Pierre purchased me, he and his family moved to a big plantation near New Orleans and brought me with them. I was Massa Pierre's personal servant, sometimes traveling with him. I made friends with his young son and he taught me how to read and write in both French and English. His father wasn't aware of it, however. Although I was living comfortable as a house servant, I still longed for my freedom. I tried to escape to a maroon settlement in the swamps, but I was caught. I made the mistake of telling another house servant my plans and he snitched on me, telling Massa Pierre. Massa Pierre was waiting on me to try to escape, and when I did, he caught me. Massa Pierre was very angry with me for trying to escape. He had me brutally whipped. I still have scars on my back from that whipping. Massa Pierre then demoted me to a field slave. After I worked in the fields for about a year, Massa Pierre sold me to a slave trader, who brought me here to South Carolina and sold me to Massa Henry."

Big Jim said, "Abraham, I didn't know you could read and write."

Abraham replied, "Yes, Big Jim, I can read and write. But I don't tell anyone; I keep it a secret. You are the first person that I have told. Look here, I'm going to show you I can write."

Abraham wrote the word freedom in the dirt. It amazed Big Jim. He had never seen a slave write before. He asked Abraham, "What do the marks in the dirt say?"

Abraham replied, "Big Jim, the letters spell the word freedom. If you escape with me up North to the 'Promised Land', I will teach you how to read and write."

Big Jim said, "No way, Abraham, running away to freedom is too risky."

Abraham replied, "Big Jim, I know running away up North sounds crazy but just keep thinking about it."

One day in early April, Big Jim and Abraham were talking inside a cabin in the slave quarters when Abraham said, "Big Jim, freedom is a wonderful thing. It means you won't have a slavemaster anymore to tell you what to do. It means you can enjoy the profit from your labor. It means you can learn to read and write without being punished."

Big Jim replied, "Abraham, I know what being free means. I was free in Africa until I was nine years old, then I was kidnapped, put on a slave ship, and brought over here."

Abraham said, "Big Jim, I didn't know that you were born in Africa. You have never mentioned this to me before. I thought that you were born on Massa Henry's plantation. Since you were once free, will you try to escape up North with me? Up North is a 'Promised Land,' a land flowing with milk and honey."

Big Jim replied, "Yes, Abraham, I am ready to escape up North with you. I want to be free like I was when I was a small boy in Africa."

Now that he had finally persuaded Big Jim to escape up North with him, Abraham decided to ask his good friend Turkey Man did he want to escape also. When Abraham asked Turkey Man about running away up North to the "Promised Land," a big smile came over his face. He said, "Yes, I want to go Abraham. I've always wanted to be a free man. I can't wait to get to that 'Promised Land.'"

Turkey Man was a very talkative field slave who was a master at imitating turkey calls. He could mimic a tom turkey, a hen, and a baby turkey. He was always imitating turkey calls; that's why people on the plantation nicknamed him Turkey Man. When he sent out calls to turkeys, they would answer him back. He was just that good.

Meanwhile, Abraham, Big Jim, and Turkey Man began to make plans for their escape. When they learned that Massa Henry was going to be down in Georgia for the whole month of May on a business trip, they decided to escape during his absence. They selected the second Saturday in May at midnight as the time they would steal away to the woods and head north. They also secretly gathered some provisions, a few bags of food, utensils, and clothing.

Soon the second Saturday in May arrived. Abraham, Big Jim, and Turkey Man were very excited to see their escape date arrive but they didn't show it.

Around 9 p.m. that Saturday night while he was sitting in his room up in the "Big House" thinking, Big Jim decided to go to the room of Tom, the butler, and tell him about the group's planned escape to the North and ask him did he want to go.

Big Jim entered Tom's room and said, "Hello, Tom, how have you been doing?"

Tom replied, "I've been doing all right, Big Jim."

Big Jim said, "Tom, guess what? Abraham, Turkey Man, and I

are planning to run away to the North tonight."

Tom replied, "What? You are running away to the North with Abraham and Turkey Man? Big Jim, you are out of your mind! Do you understand what you are saying? You better not run away with Abraham, I'm telling you now. Abraham is a troublemaker; he will get you in big trouble. I've been watching you talk to Abraham down in the slave quarters. Don't talk to him! Stay away from him! He's slick; he will fill your head with bad ideas that will get you in trouble. He is always talking that 'old freedom talk.' Talking about he is going to escape up North to the Promised Land. Abraham is also very lazy. He is always trying to avoid work, and always telling Mister Jack, the overseer, that he is sick. I heard Massa Henry tell Mr. Jack the other day that he is going to sell that lazy Abraham the next time the slave trader comes through. He says Abraham is a bad influence on the other slaves."

Big Jim said, "Tom, you just don't understand Abraham. He wants to be free! Tom, I want to be free too! I'm tired of being a slave."

Tom replied, "Big Jim, you have it made here on the plantation. You are not a field slave. You don't have to work from can see to can't see in the cotton fields. You are a house servant. All you have to do is drive Massa Henry around in the carriage and keep him laughing with your funny stories. You have it made and don't know it. You are also Massa Henry's favorite slave. He treats you better than the rest of us. He lets you go places with him. You go to horse races, fox hunts, and to town with him. He doesn't allow the rest of us those privileges. You are walking in tall cotton, Big Jim, but you don't realize it. You have it made."

Big Jim said, "Yes, Tom, I am treated better than you all are, but I am still not free. I am a slave; I want to be free; that is why I am going to run away, to get my freedom. Tom, it doesn't matter whether we work in the fields or in the 'Big House' or in the black-smith shop, we are still slaves."

The truth that Big Jim said irritated Tom. He responded with, "Big Jim, do you understand the danger and risk in running away? If you are caught by the slave patrol, things won't be the same. You will be whipped or even punished worse! You will lose your privileged house position and be demoted to the fields. You might even be sold to a cruel slavemaster somewhere. Big Jim, have you ever seen Abraham with his shirt off? It is an ugly sight to see. His back is all scarred up. He was cruelly beaten when he was caught trying to run away from his master down in Louisiana."

Big Jim said, "Tom, freedom isn't free! You have to take a risk if you ever want to be free, and I'm going to take that risk. Do you want to take that risk, Tom, and run away with us?"

Tom said, "What did you say Big Jim? You asked me to run away and risk getting caught when I have it made here on this plantation? You have to be kidding, Big Jim! I have no reason to want to run away. I eat the same food that Massa Henry eats. This morning for breakfast I had ham and eggs, hot-buttered biscuits, sorghum molasses, and milk. I'm eating high on the hog. This morning for breakfast the field slaves had grits, hoecake bread, and fatback meat. I live in the 'Big House' with Massa Henry. I don't live down in the cabins with the field gang. I wear the same clothes that Massa Henry wears. I don't wear a cotton shirt and pants and 'Brogan shoes' like the field slaves. I got it made. I'm Massa Henry's slave. He's the richest white man in these parts. Massa Henry makes sure that all of his slaves have clothes to wear, shoes to wear, and enough food to eat. Massa Henry is a good white man; he's not evil like Mr. Travis of the Pine Hill Plantation. Big Jim, if you are asking me to leave Massa Henry, 'this good white man,' you are out of your mind. I'm going to stay right here on Massa Henry's plantation."

Big Jim replied, "Tom, whatever you do is your personal business but I'm going to run away up North to the 'Promised Land.'"

Tom said, "Big Jim, you better not run away; I'm telling you now! You better stay on this plantation. Abraham and Turkey Man are troublemakers. If you run away with them, they will get you in trouble."

Big Jim replied, "Tom, I have already made up my mind to escape with Abraham and Turkey Man. We are going to make it up North to freedom, you'll see."

At midnight Abraham, Big Jim, and Turkey Man met at a prearranged spot in the woods. They were ready to begin their trip north to freedom. Abraham was chosen to be the leader of the little group. After talking quietly for a few minutes, the little group headed north. The date was May of 1829.

Abraham, Big Jim, and Turkey Man were keenly aware that they were about to attempt a very dangerous and risky venture. They knew that they had to be careful; one mistake could mean capture and return to slavery or even worse. They knew that they would have to travel mostly at night, and through woods and back ways as much as possible. They knew that going through the slave states would be the most dangerous part of their journey, but when they reached the free states they knew they still couldn't afford to relax.

The first week of the runaway slaves' journey up through South Carolina went so smooth and easy that it lulled them into a false sense of security. They became lax and dropped their guard and it got them into trouble. This is what happened: one morning they made a fire to cook some fish that they had caught and the fire attracted the attention of two hunters nearby.

The two hunters were on top of a tree-covered hill when they saw smoke rising from down in the valley. They eased down the hill to investigate the smoke, but their path was blocked by a creek.

Across the creek in a little clearing, they saw three Negroes sitting around a fire eating. The sight surprised and delighted the two hunters. One said to the other, "By golly, Bill, look at those three Negroes. I bet they are runaway slaves! If we capture them, we can get a good price for them, more money than we can make hunting. Look at that big one there. He's very tall and powerfully built. He's worth lots of bucks. Let's creep back up the hill, get our guns and dogs, walk up stream a bit, cross the creek where it is shallow, and then surprise and capture those Negroes."

In the meantime, Abraham began to sense danger, with the three sitting out in the open around a fire. He said, "Big Jim, Turkey Man, we are through eating, let's get out of here. The smoke from the fire can attract attention."

The three picked up their sacks and began walking in the woods. They had walked about a half hour when they heard the distant sound of dogs barking and men talking. The noise put fear into them and they began running through the woods. After about a half hour of running from the hunters and their dogs, Abraham said to the others, "If we can't shake these men off of our trail, we are in big trouble. They have dogs that will follow our scent until we drop."

The three continued to run with the dogs in hot pursuit of them. Eventually, they came to a stream, which gave Abraham an idea. He said, "Big Jim and Turkey Man, after we cross this stream, we are going to rub our bodies with the onions in this sack and I believe the onions' smell will 'throw the dogs off our scent', and so confuse them that they won't be able to follow our trail."

Sure enough, the idea worked to perfection. When the hunters crossed the stream, their dogs became confused by the onion smell and were unable to follow the escaped slaves' scent. One hunter said to the other, "Tom, darn it, I believe those three Negroes have gotten away from us. I thought we would be able to capture them and make us some money. But it smells like they used onions to confuse our dogs. We don't know which way they went. Darn it, our money has gotten away! But what those runaway slaves don't know is once you cross this stream, you are going to run into swampland, and it doesn't matter whether you go north, east, or west. When those runaway slaves travel about five more miles they are going to run right into the largest swamp they have ever seen, and they won't make it out of there alive."

Meanwhile, Abraham, Big Jim, and Turkey Man had arrived on the edge of the swamp. After looking at the edge of the huge swamp, Abraham decided that it was best for them to spend the night where they were.

In the morning Abraham, Big Jim, and Turkey Man entered the huge swamp and began their travel through it. Snakes and other dangers lurked in the murky waters and dense vegetation, but thanks to Abraham's knowledge of swamps that he had learned down in Louisiana, the three picked their way through the treacherous swamp and made it out alive. It took five days for them to make it out of the huge swamp.

The three continued their journey up through South Carolina. One day they entered an area that Abraham said contained quick sand. He warned Big Jim and Turkey Man to be careful and watch their steps. However, after a few hours of being cautious, Turkey Man became lax and began laughing and talking when suddenly he stepped into a spot of quicksand. The more he struggled to get out of the quicksand the deeper he sank into it. Unable to get out of the quicksand, Turkey Man panicked and began screaming and hollering and moving around. Abraham told him to be still, because the more he moved around, the deeper he would sink in the quicksand. Abraham then tried to pull Turkey Man out of the quicksand but he couldn't do it. Big Jim also tried to pull Turkey Man out of the quicksand but he couldn't do it either. The situation grew desperate when Turkey Man sank deeper in the quicksand, up to his shoulders. Big Jim, realizing that Turkey Man would soon be swallowed up, grabbed him again by the arm and pulled with all of his great strength. Suddenly there was a loud popping noise, which was the sound of the quicksand releasing Turkey Man. Big Jim's super second effort had saved Turkey Man's life.

By late June the three had traveled through South Carolina and were in North Carolina. They continued to move up through North Carolina, traveling most of the time at night through woods and backcountry to avoid towns and people.

One day while traveling the three came upon a cozy, little farm tucked away in the woods, surrounded by cornfields and orchards. They were so hungry that they decided to take a risk and get some ears of corn from a cornfield of the little farm. They began pulling ears of corn from the cornstalks, but they made a little too much noise, which aroused the attention of the old farmer working in the barn nearby. Upon hearing the noise, the old farmer came out of the barn with his rifle and began walking toward the cornfield to investigate the noise he had just heard. It looked like the three would be caught. But Turkey Man saved the day. He began gobbling like a tom turkey and he sounded so much like a tom turkey that the old farmer was completely fooled. Instead of continuing on with his investigation of the noise in the cornfield, he turned around, smiled, and walked back toward the barn thinking to himself, "There is no one out there. That noise is that old tom turkey calling his hens again and moving around in the cornfield."

After the narrow escape with the old farmer, the little group was more cautious when it took food from places.

In the meantime, Abraham, Big Jim, and Turkey Man continued to move on up through North Carolina and by the first week in August they were in Virginia.

While traveling up through Virginia, the three lost their sense of direction one cloudy night. To keep from wandering around aimlessly, they remained in the woods where they were. The next night the sky cleared, and Abraham was able to locate the North Star and use it as a guide. After regaining their sense of direction, the three continued to push on northward and by mid-September, they were in northern Virginia.

Early one morning in northern Virginia, the three came upon an old colored man who was gathering firewood in the woods. They approached him with caution, and when they were within hearing distance from him, Abraham began singing the spiritual song "Steal Away to Jesus." After a few minutes of singing the song, Abraham stopped singing it. Within a few minutes the old colored man began singing "Steal Away to Jesus", and then he stopped singing it and beckoned the little group toward him. He had understood that the song was coded and the three men were slaves running away to freedom. He was as happy to see them as they were to see him. He told them his name was George and that he was a free Negro. The three then introduced themselves to him. After they had gotten acquainted with each other, the old man asked, "What part of Virginia are you escaping from?"

Abraham answered, "We are escaping from a plantation near Charleston, South Carolina."

The old man said, "You have traveled all the way up here from South Carolina. Well, blow me down, I can't believe it! You are very blessed to make it all the way up here. The Lord is looking out for you."

Abraham replied, "You are right, Sir. We are blessed."

The old man said, "You are traveling through a very dangerous part of Virginia. It's best to travel only at night because slave catchers are lurking around. Remain here in the woods today, and to-night I will bring you some food. I am taking a big risk helping runaway slaves, but I'm going to do it anyway."

True to his word, that night around 9:00 the old man brought them plenty of food to eat. He also told them how to reach the house of a white man who helped runaway slaves.

The old man said, "You are about twenty miles from the Potomac River. There is a white man named John Houston who lives near this river. If you go to his house he will ferry you across the river and help you reach Pennsylvania, a free state. If you follow this trail, it will lead you right to his house. His house is located where this trail cross another trail, the third house on the right. His house has a lawn jockey in front of it and trees in the yard. On the side of the house is a quilt hanging on a clothesline. The quilt has five crosses embroidered on it. The cross represents a crossing point, where the trails cross each other. The lawn jockey and the quilt secretly show a coded message which is 'runaway slaves are welcomed and helped here where the trails cross each other.' When you get to his house go around to the back door and knock five times in succession; then knock five more times in succession. The ten knocks on the door are a coded message. When Mr. Houston hears the ten knocks he will let you in. Tell him Old George sent you to him. Make sure no one sees you knock on his door. Wait until dusk-dark before you knock on his door."

Abraham, Big Jim, and Turkey Man thanked Old George for helping them and told him good-bye. They then pushed on toward the Potomac River and the house of John Houston, the runaway slave helper.

The three didn't have any problems locating the house of John Houston. They saw the lawn jockey and the quilt hanging on the clothesline just as Old George had said. Around dusk-dark they left the woods where they had been hiding, and went around to the back of Houston's house. Abraham knocked on the door five times in succession; then he knocked five more times in succession. A tall, middle aged, white man and a dog came to the door. Abraham said, "Old George sent us to you. We are runaway slaves."

The white man studied the three runaway slaves for a minute, then he smiled and said, "Yes, I know Old George. He helps runaway slaves. You all come in, welcome to my house. Old George probably told you fellows that my name is John Houston and I help runaway slaves."

Next, Abraham, Big Jim, and Turkey Man introduced themselves to him. After which, John Houston asked, "What plantation from around here did you escape from?"

Abraham answered, "We escaped from a plantation near Charleston, South Carolina, Sir."

John Houston said, "Whew, my, oh my, you fellows have traveled all the way up here from South Carolina. That's a long ways from here. You are very fortunate to have made it up here to northern Virginia."

Abraham replied, "Yessah, we sure are very fortunate."

John Houston said, "I know you fellows are tired and hungry. We have plenty of food and clothes. After you eat, you can change clothes, and sleep in the cellar. Tomorrow night I will ferry you across the Potomac River and then take you to a friend's house in Maryland. My friend will take you across the state of Maryland to freedom in Pennsylvania."

The following night John Houston ferried Abraham, Big Jim, and Turkey Man across the Potomac River. Then, they were taken to a man named Paul Hamilton's house. He told them he was going to take them across the state of Maryland to a friend's house in Pennsylvania. The next morning the trip began. Abraham, Big Jim, and Turkey Man climbed into a wagon and were covered up, disguised as freight. After three weeks on the road, the group reached its destination, a farm near Harrisburg, Pennsylvania. The date was October of 1829.

Abraham, Big Jim, and Turkey Man had finally made it to the "Promised Land." They were some very happy fellows to be in a free state. Their roughly 700 miles journey from Charleston, South Carolina to Harrisburg, Pennsylvania had taken five months. Their journey had been filled with dangers of all kinds, including slave catchers, the slave patrol, treacherous swamps, quick sand, hunger, and bad weather. But due to their courage, determination, and quick wits, they had made it up North to the "Promised Land."

The owner of the farm where Abraham, Big Jim, and Turkey Man were taken to was a man named Joseph Coffin. He was a tall, fat, friendly white man, a Quaker and an abolitionist, and he loved a good laugh. He was fascinated by Big Jim's great height and size. He told Abraham, Big Jim, and Turkey Man that he needed laborers on his farm and if they worked for him, he would pay them wages and provide them with a cabin to live in. The offer sounded good to the three and they gladly accepted it.

About two weeks after their arrival on Mr. Joseph Coffin's farm, the three decided to celebrate their escape up North to the "Promised Land." They told Mr. Coffin about their planned celebration. He laughed and said it was a good idea for them to celebrate their newfound freedom. He provided them with plenty of food and a barrel of apple cider for their celebration.

Also, Abraham invited some guests, black men and women, from surrounding farms to celebrate with them.

The "Big Celebration" to mark Abraham, Big Jim, and Turkey Man's escape to freedom took place in a large cabin on Mr. Coffin's farm. It was the celebration to end all celebrations. It began early on a Saturday night and lasted until the break of day. Abraham, Big Jim, Turkey Man, and their guests truly enjoyed themselves and had lots of fun. They ate and drank to their hearts were content. They danced, sang songs, told jokes and stories, and had a very good time. Big Jim had everyone falling out laughing with his funny animal stories. Turkey Man entertained everyone with his variety of turkey calls. He imitated the call of a tom turkey; he imitated the call of a hen turkey; and he imitated the call of a baby turkey. Turkey Man got so carried away with his turkey calls that Abraham and Big Jim had to tell him to be quiet. Abraham entertained everyone with his skillful mimicking of people on the Mills' plantation. He had everyone roaring with laughter with his skillful mimicking of Tom the butler and Massa Henry the slavemaster. He acted, walked, and talked just like them. The highlight of the celebration, however, was Abraham's singing a song that he had created especially for the occasion, it was called "I Know Massa Henry Is Going to Miss Me, Now That I Am Gone." Big Jim and Turkey Man thought the song was very funny because they knew that Abraham would be the last slave that Massa Henry would miss. When Abraham had been on the plantation, he had gained a reputation for being lazy, rebellious, and a troublemaker. As a result of his bad reputation, Massa Henry would never miss Abraham. His only regret would be he didn't get the chance to sell him.

Meanwhile, when Massa Henry had returned from Georgia, he was shocked to learn that Abraham, Big Jim, and Turkey Man had run away from the plantation. He prided himself on being a good slavemaster and it was hard for him to understand why any of his slaves would run away. This was the first time that slaves had run away from his plantation.

Massa Henry blamed himself for his slaves running away. He knew he should have listened to Tom. Tom had told him that

Abraham was a troublemaker and was always talking about he was going to escape up North to the "Promised Land." Tom had also told him that Abraham was filling Big Jim's ears with freedom talk. But he hadn't taken Tom's information serious enough. He never believed that Abraham would be able to persuade Big Jim and Turkey Man to run away with him. He now realized that he should have sold that lazy and rebellious rascal Abraham before he had ruined Big Jim with all that freedom talk.

Losing Big Jim really upset Massa Henry. He had gotten used to laughing at his funny stories, and he missed him. He thought about sending a professional slave catcher to find Big Jim and bring him back, but he changed his mind.

During the winter of 1829-30, Massa Henry missed hearing Big Jim's funny stories, and by spring he had changed his mind again and had decided to hire someone to find Big Jim and bring him back. The person he hired to find Big Jim and bring him back was the famous slave catcher Daniel Hayes.

Although Massa Henry wanted his slave Big Jim back, he didn't want him returned to him physically injured. He, therefore, gave the slave catcher Daniel Hayes strict orders on how to deal with Big Jim. The reason Massa Henry didn't want Big Jim physically harmed was because he had been his favorite slave and had also brought laughter back into his sister's life. Massa Henry hadn't forgotten that.

Massa Henry told the slave catcher Daniel Hayes to bring Big Jim back, but if he refused to come back, not to physically force him to come back, instead tell him he could remain free under a stipulation. The stipulation was this: Big Jim could remain free up North but if he ever was caught sleeping in the yard outside his house, alone, rather than inside of it, he could be reenslaved.

The slave catcher Daniel Hayes had become famous for his ability to catch runaway slaves. He knew all the tricks of the trade and possessed the uncanny ability to follow a cold trail. In April of 1830 he and his three sons began their search to find Big Jim and bring him back. Although the trail of the three escaped slaves was nearly a year old, Daniel Hayes felt confident that he could follow it. From years of experience, he had learned to think like a runaway slave would think. He figured the three runaway slaves had headed north, traveling through wooded areas and backcountry. He, therefore, began to search the backcountry in South Carolina for someone who had seen the three runaway slaves. After about a month of searching, Daniel Hayes and his sons hit pay dirt. They located the two hunters who had chased the three runaway slaves but had been unable to catch them. The two hunters told Daniel Hayes that they had seen three Negroes matching his descriptions, and they had chased them but they had lost their trail. Continuing his search for information in South Carolina, Daniel Hayes hit pay dirt again. He talked to an old man who remembered last June seeing three Negroes in the woods that matched his descriptions. The old man told Daniel Hayes that one of the three Negroes was a giant, the biggest Negro that he had ever seen in his life. The old man also told Daniel Hayes that the three Negroes were headed northward, confirming what he had figured. In southern Virginia Daniel Hayes hit pay dirt for the third time. A woman told him that three runaway slaves matching his descriptions had taken melons out of her melon patch, but had disappeared so quickly that her husband was unable to chase them. From his conversation with the woman, Daniel Hayes figured that the three runaway slaves had probably headed to freedom in Pennsylvania or New York. While searching for the three runaway slaves in southeastern Pennsylvania, Daniel Hayes hit pay dirt for the fourth time. A man told him that he had seen three Negroes that matched his descriptions working on a farm near Harrisburg, Pennsylvania. Daniel Hayes and his three sons soon located the farm and sure enough they saw the three runaway slaves working in a field. They then began to develop a strategy on how to capture them. They planned to sell Abraham and Turkey Man. Big Jim would be returned to Massa Henry.

Meanwhile, Abraham, Big Jim, and Turkey Man enjoyed their newfound freedom on Mr. Coffin's farm in Pennsylvania. They were getting paid for their labor and were excited about it. One morning in early September of 1830, as they worked in a field a cheerful farmer came up to them and said with a smile, "Good morning, fellows, how are you all doing?"

Abraham, Big Jim, and Turkey Man replied, "Good morning to you, Sir."

The cheerful farmer said, "I am experiencing a little trouble fellows. My wagon has gotten stuck in a mud hole about two miles down the road, and I would be very thankful if you would help me get my wagon out of it."

Big Jim said, "No problem, Sir. We'll help you get it out of the mud hole."

Abraham said, "We are very sorry, Sir, but we just don't have the time to help you."

Turkey Man said, "Ah, come on Abraham, we have the time to help this nice man get his wagon out of the mud hole."

Abraham said, "We are sorry, Sir, but our boss, Mr. Coffin, doesn't like for us to leave the field without his permission."

The cheerful farmer replied, "You mean to tell me, you won't help a poor farmer get his wagon out of a mud hole? Shame on you!"

Abraham said, "Sorry, Sir, but Mr. Coffin wouldn't like it if we left the field without his permission."

The cheerful farmer said with a sly smile, "Maybe you fellows will help me next time. Thank you, anyway."

After the cheerful farmer had left, Abraham told Big Jim and Turkey Man that they had to start being more careful with strangers. He said, "Big Jim, Turkey Man, we didn't know who that stranger was. He could have been a slave catcher for all we know. We are runaway slaves; we have to be careful with strangers."

Once again Abraham had saved Big Jim and Turkey Man, because the cheerful farmer they had just talked to was Daniel Hayes, the famous slave catcher himself, who was a master of disguise. He had disguised himself as a cheerful farmer to lure the three runaway slaves from the field so he and his sons could capture them. His disguise had been so good that Big Jim and Turkey Man were completely fooled, but Abraham had been suspicious of him.

When Daniel Hayes got back to the woods, he told his sons that the strategy to bait the three runaway slaves into a trap had failed. He then decided to catch Big Jim alone and try to capture him.

One morning a few days later, Big Jim had gone to a general store in the town of Harrisburg to buy some goods and was on his way back home when he was suddenly surrounded by three men on horseback. Within a few minutes, a fourth man in a wagon rode up and joined them. The man in the wagon said, "Big Jim, you are surrounded, and there is no way out. We came to take you back to your slavemaster, Henry Mills. So get into this wagon and we will be on our way."

Big Jim replied, "I don't know who you all are but I'm not going to get into that wagon."

Daniel Hayes son Jeff, who was mean and quick-tempered, said, "Well, well, just listen to the Negro talk! He says that he is not going to do what a white man tells him to do anymore. A little freedom has gone to his head and got him acting uppity. Now, listen here, Big Negro, you had better get into this wagon if you know what's good for you."

Big Jim replied, "I'm not going to get into that wagon."

Daniel Hayes, seeing that Big Jim was going to resist capture and they would have to use physical force to get him into the wagon, said to him, "Big Jim, you are a mighty lucky Negro to have such a kind slavemaster. He told us not to harm you. Otherwise, we would force you into this wagon, put chains on you, and deliver you to your slavemaster. However, he said that you could remain free under a stipulation. You had better listen, and listen well to this stipulation. It says: you can remain free up North, but if you are ever caught sleeping in the yard outside your house, alone, instead of inside it, you can be reenslaved."

After Big Jim had been told his stipulation, Daniel Hayes and his three sons rode off, headed back down South.

The incident with the slave catchers bothered Big Jim. When he told Abraham about it, Abraham said, "Big Jim, I keep telling you and Turkey Man to be watchful at all times. We are runaway slaves and our freedom can be taken away at any moment. Be careful going to town alone. And furthermore, you need to always be aware of that stipulation. Never go to sleep in the yard outside your house, alone, otherwise you may end up one day back in slavery. Remember to always be careful and stay alert."

Big Jim replied, "You are right Abraham. I need to always be careful and alert. I'm going to try to always be like that."

After thinking for a while, Big Jim said, "Abraham, I believe that the cheerful farmer who tried to get us to help him get his wagon out of the mud hole last week was the leader of that slave catching gang. He talked just like their leader."

Abraham replied, "Big Jim, I bet you are right. Sometimes clever slave catchers use disguises to fool people. That's the reason I keep telling you and Turkey Man to be cautious with strangers. You don't know them; they don't have to be who they appear to be."

Big Jim said, "You are right, Abraham. I need to be more cautious with strangers. The cheerful farmer completely fooled me. I thought he was for real. From now on I'm going to be more cautious with strangers."

Abraham replied, "Big Jim, I don't feel safe around here anymore. I think we need to move on to another town."

Abraham told Mr. Coffin, the owner of the farm, about how a gang of slave catchers had tried to capture Big Jim and how the leader of the gang had tried to lure them into a trap. After listening to their story, Mr. Coffin said, "I thought you fellows were safe here but these two incidents prove me wrong. It is probably best that you move on to another town. I have a cousin named Randolph Penn who owns a farm near Philadelphia. You can go there and work for him. He will be glad to have good workers like you to help him on his farm. I will write him a letter and tell him about you."

In November Joseph Coffin took Abraham, Big Jim, and Turkey Man to his cousin's farm near Philadelphia. The three found Randolph Penn to be friendly and jolly like his cousin but not as talkative. By the spring of the next year, 1831, the three had adjusted to life on the Penn farm and had made some friends in the black section of Philadelphia.

In late May, the three were invited to a big dance in Philadelphia. At the dance Big Jim met a pretty young lady named Lucille with whom he danced with all night. She was twenty-one years old and single. Big Jim really liked her and told her so. After the dance he asked her if he could come to her home and get better acquainted with her. She said yes. Once Big Jim and Lucille began courting, their attraction to each other grew stronger and stronger. All summer and fall they had lots of fun together attending dances, picnics, and other social events. Lucille had never met a man like

Big Jim, and she was overwhelmed by his charm, talent, and sense of humor. She enjoyed listening to him sing, play the banjo, and tell funny stories. Most of all, however, she enjoyed dancing with him at the dances they attended. By the spring of the next year, Big Jim and Lucille had fallen deeply in love with each other. That fall they were married.

After the wedding, Big Jim and Lucille moved into their own cabin on Mr. Penn's farm. Mr. Penn helped the happy couple get started by providing them with food, clothing, and some furniture. Big Jim and Lucille worked hard on Mr. Penn's farm and were thrifty with their money. In August of 1833 their first child was born. They named him Matthew.

Abraham and Turkey Man also continued to live on Mr. Penn's farm, working as laborers. During some of his spare time, Abraham taught Big Jim, Turkey Man, and Lucille how to read and write. In July of 1835 Turkey Man got married. He then left Mr. Penn's farm and moved with his new wife to the city of Philadelphia and found him a job there. In August Abraham also left the farm and went to live in Philadelphia.

In March of 1837 Big Jim and Lucille had their second child, a girl. She was named Marie.

The second child made the small cabin crowded and Big Jim and Lucille began looking for a small farm to buy with the money they had saved. In May their problem was solved when they brought five acres of land very cheaply from Mr. Penn. He also helped them to build a house and gave them hogs and chickens to raise.

Big Jim and Lucille were a hard working, industrious couple. By 1845 they had turned their five acres of land into a prosperous farm. They had a pen full of hogs, they had a large number of chickens in the yard, and they had a half dozen cows and a bull in the pasture. Their garden contained a variety of vegetables, their fields produced an abundance of potatoes and corn, and their orchards produced plenty apples and peaches.

Lucille often made these apples and peaches into delicious pies to sell. Her pies were so good that people for miles around wanted to sample them.

Once a week Big Jim would take a wagonload of these pies into the city of Philadelphia to sell. His great sense of humor would attract lots of customers to his wagon. They would gather around his wagon to listen to his funny stories and after bursting their sides laughing at his funny stories, they would generally buy some of his delicious pies. Big Jim made nice money selling these pies. Many people looked forward to him coming to town so they could enjoy his funny stories and eat his delicious pies.

In 1848 Abraham left Philadelphia and moved to New York. He was now very involved with the Underground Railroad, helping escaped slaves reach the "Promised Land" of the North. Of course, he was the same old Abraham, full of fun and always talking plenty smack. He hadn't got married yet, but he said he was working on it.

Turkey Man still lived in Philadelphia. He was doing well with his wife and five children, working as a laborer for a rich white merchant. Big Jim often visited him when he was in Philadelphia. Of course, he was the same old Turkey Man, still imitating turkey calls. He was well liked and well known in his community; he often amused his neighbors with his variety of turkey calls.

In 1851 Big Jim turned fifty-three years old. He was now a successful farmer and a happy family man. His wife Lucille was forty-one; his son Matthew was eighteen; and his daughter Marie was fourteen. With a thriving farm and a nice family, Big Jim was happy and content. He had come a long way since arriving in Pennsylvania over twenty years ago.

Meanwhile, down in South Carolina, Massa Henry had grown old and sick. He didn't have much longer to live. Despite his sickness, he constantly talked about Big Jim and his funny stories. One day in March of 1852, he told his daughter Laura that he wanted to see Big Jim. He said, "Laura, I want to see Big Jim so he can tell me some of his funny stories. I know it has been a long time since I've seen him, but I still want to hear some of his funny stories."

Laura replied, "Daddy, it has been almost twenty-three years since Big Jim escaped from this plantation. It will be very difficult to find him now. He could be anywhere or even dead. And furthermore, I thought you said that he could remain free up North."

Massa Henry said, "Yes, I did say that Big Jim could remain free up North, but under a stipulation. The stipulation says if he is ever caught sleeping in his yard outside his house, alone, instead of inside it, he can be reenslaved."

Laura replied, "Oh, I didn't know that Daddy."

Massa Henry said, "Laura, grant an old, sick man his wish. I want to see Big Jim so I can laugh at some of his funny stories. I believe the famous slave catcher Daniel Hayes can find him and bring him back here."

When Laura talked to Daniel Hayes, he was somewhat hesitant about trying to find Big Jim. He said, "Laura, it will be difficult to find him. It has been over twenty years since I last saw him in Pennsylvania and he could be anywhere up North now or even dead. But I will try to find him and bring him back. Henry wants to listen to his funny stories so much."

In late March of 1852 Daniel Hayes and his three sons began their search to find Big Jim and bring him back to South Carolina. Daniel Hayes figured that if Big Jim were still alive, he would probably be in Pennsylvania or New York. He and his sons, therefore, headed to Pennsylvania. When they arrived in Pennsylvania, they went to the town of Harrisburg, but the people there said they hadn't seen him in over twenty years. After searching for weeks throughout Pennsylvania, they still were unable to find anyone who knew exactly where he was. One man in the town of Reading, Pennsylvania said that when he was visiting his cousin in Philadelphia, he had heard people talking about a giant Negro who told funny stories. Another man in the town of Easton, Pennsylvania said that he had seen a giant Negro named Big Jim selling pies and telling funny stories when he was in Philadelphia about five years ago. The two descriptions about a giant Negro who told funny stories caused Daniel Hayes to believe that he was on the right track. He decided to search for Big Jim in Philadelphia. He went to the black section of Philadelphia but the Negroes he talked to had never heard of a giant Negro named Big Jim who told funny stories. He continued to search and one day he talked to a young Negro man who said that he had never heard of Big Jim but his face showed he had heard of him. Daniel Hayes was an alert man, and he believed the young Negro man was trying to hide something.

Suddenly it dawned on Daniel Hayes that his Southern drawl and Southern way of dressing were causing the Negroes to be suspicious of him. He thought to himself, "There is more than one way to skin a cat."

One day a few days later in the black section of Philadelphia, a well-dressed and charming white businessman warmly greeted an old Negro couple who were sitting on their front porch. He said with a warm smile, "Good morning, Uncle and Auntie, how are you all doing this beautiful day?"

The old Negro couple replied, "We are doing fine, Sir."

The well-dressed and charming white businessman said, "Uncle and Auntie, I hope you all can help me. I'm looking for a giant Negro man named Big Jim who tells funny stories. I owe him some money for buying a wagonload of his delicious pies, and I want to pay him. I was told that he lives somewhere on this street."

The old Negro man laughed heartily and said, "Mister, you got to be talking about Big Jim. He doesn't live on this street. He lives outside town on a farm about fifteen miles from here."

The well-dressed and charming white businessman smiled broadly and said, "Uncle and Auntie, you have been so helpful. Thank you very much. I'm going out to Big Jim's farm so I can pay him the money that I owe him. Here, Uncle and Auntie, take this $20 for being so nice and helpful to me. Go to the store and buy yourselves something."

That afternoon Daniel Hayes told his sons that his disguise as a well-dressed and charming businessman had worked to perfection. They found Big Jim's farm that evening. He and his family were working in a cornfield. After finding where Big Jim lived, Daniel Hayes and his three sons began devising a strategy on how to capture him.

Meanwhile, the next day, Saturday, Big Jim and his family were eating breakfast when Lucille said, "Big Jim, the children and I are going to town this afternoon. But before we go, I am going to cook you a very special dinner. It is my way of expressing my love for you and my appreciation for your hard work this summer."

Big Jim replied, "I appreciate that, Honey. You know I love good food and you are the best cook around. But before I eat your special dinner this afternoon, I'm going to do some work around the farm."

When Big Jim came up to the house from the cornfield that afternoon at 1 o'clock, he could smell the aroma of good food cooking. He was very hungry after working hard all morning in the cornfield. Lucille said, "Big Jim, the kids and I are getting ready to go to town. The food is on the table here in the yard; enjoy it."

Big Jim sat down at the table in the yard. It was loaded with food that smelled so good. On the table was a meal fit for a king: finger licking good fried chicken; slices of delicious hickory smoked ham; good old turnip greens, peas, and squash; good old mashed potatoes and gravy; good old egg cornbread that was baked to a golden brown; a mouth-watering peach cobbler; and a pitcher filled with ice cold water from the well. The food was so good to Big Jim. He ate until his stomach was filled. After he finished eating, he felt so sleepy. He started to go into the house and go to sleep but he just didn't feel like walking to the house. So he laid down in the yard under a big oak tree and went to sleep.

Meanwhile, Daniel Hayes and his sons had been carefully watching Big Jim's house from the woods. They had seen his wife and kids leave in the wagon. When they saw him sleeping in the yard outside his house, alone, instead of inside it, they chuckled with delight. He was in the kind of vulnerable position they had waited for. Suddenly, they swooped down on him and tried to put chains on him. But they awakened Big Jim and he fought them with all of his strength. He was still a good man at fifty-four, big and strong, and they were unable to subdue him. Finally, Daniel Hayes' son Jeff put a pistol to Big Jim's head and said to him, "Big Negro, if you don't give up, I'm going to blow your brains out."

Big Jim knowing that he had angered the slave catchers with his resistance, and they were ready to kill him, said, "Okay, I give up."

As they were putting the chains on him, Big Jim suddenly realized that he had violated Massa Henry's stipulation. He had gone to sleep in the yard outside his house, alone, and was therefore subject to reenslavement. With the passing of time, he had become less and less cautious, and had eventually forgotten about the stipulation. Now he was paying the price for not being alert. Abraham had warned him years ago to always be alert and to watch out for slave catchers. But he had not done that. He had been lulled into a false sense of security by years of peace and prosperity. At first he had been alert but as the years passed he had become more and more complacent. Finally, he had gotten so complacent that he had forgotten altogether about remaining alert and had gone to sleep. Now he was paying the price of reenslavement for not remaining alert.

Meanwhile, Big Jim arrived on the Mills' plantation in late August of 1852. He had been gone from South Carolina for twenty-three years. When he saw Massa Henry, he had changed a lot. He was no longer the stocky, jolly, healthy-looking man he once was, instead he was frail, sick, and despondent. However, he was glad to see Big Jim. He asked him to tell him some of his funny stories and, of course, he did. The funny story about "The Courtship of Brer Monkey and Sister Elephant" caused Massa Henry to burst into laughter. He laughed so hard that his daughter Laura had to come and pat him on the back to keep him from choking. Massa Henry hadn't had a good laugh like that in a very long time.

When Big Jim drove around the Mills' plantation in the carriage, he saw that things had changed a great deal since his escape in May of 1829. The productivity and physical condition of the plantation had declined. The mood of the slaves had also changed; they rarely laughed like they used to in the old days, instead they were sullen and sad-looking. Some of the slaves also had died, including Tom the butler, and Elvira, a maid.

The slaves on the plantation that remembered Big Jim were happy to see him again, especially Old Ben, the blacksmith, and Bessie, the cook. But on the other hand, they regretted that he had been reenslaved.

One evening Bessie, the cook, came to Big Jim with a sad look on her face. She said in a hushed tone, "Big Jim, come go to the smokehouse with me. I have something I want to tell you."

Big Jim replied, "Okay, Bessie, let's go to the smokehouse."

Inside the smokehouse, where the meat was stored, Bessie said, "Big Jim, Massa Henry is very sick, and he isn't able to run the plantation anymore. He also doesn't know what is going on around here anymore. His son-in-law, Nathan, runs the plantation, and that is why it is in such bad shape. Massa Henry has a mysterious illness that keeps him in bed. This mysterious illness saps his strength, makes him cough until he is out of breath, and causes him to have chills and fever at night. The doctors don't know what it is, and they can't cure it. They expect him to die soon. And if he dies, his son-in-law Nathan plans to sell the plantation and all of us to Mr. Travis and move down to Georgia. You know how mean and evil Mr. Travis is. He's the worst slavemaster in these parts. Big Jim, if Massa Henry dies like Dr. Dunn expects him to, we are in big trouble. I heard slaves are treated real cruel on Mr. Travis plantation and they die young. They don't get enough food to eat; they are whipped for any little thing that they do wrong; they sometimes don't get shoes in the wintertime and have to tie rags around their feet for shoes; and they are worked like mules. You know he beat a slave to death years ago for running away. They say Old Man Travis said that the slaves on Henry Mills' plantation have been getting off easy for a long time, but when he buys them he's going to show them what slavery is really like."

Big Jim replied, "Bessie, if Massa Henry dies, we are in for a rough time. Old Man Travis is an evil man and he will treat us especially mean. You know his saying is 'Kill a mule, buy a mule; kill a slave, buy a slave.'"

Big Jim thought for a while, then he said, "Bessie, I believe I can cure Massa Henry. When I was around fifteen years old I saw Uncle Charlie cure some slaves who had the same kind of sickness that

Massa Henry has. Uncle Charlie went down to the swamp and brought back a plant that had a long root. He made a tea from the root of the plant and cured the slaves with it. I still remember how the plant looked. If I can find it, I believe I can cure Massa Henry with it. Curing him will prevent us from being sold to old, evil Mr. Travis. I have to find that plant."

The next day Big Jim told Massa Henry that if he could find a certain plant, he believed he could cure him of his illness. Massa Henry was skeptical at first, but when Big Jim told him that Uncle Charlie had used the plant to cure some slaves who had the same illness that he had, he began to believe. Finally, Big Jim was able to convince him that he could cure him if he could find the plant.

Subsequently, Big Jim and Bessie began to look in the swamps for the plant. They looked every day in September and October for the plant, hours and hours, but they couldn't find it. One day in early November they went deep into a dangerous and treacherous swamp and by chance Big Jim spotted the plant and became very excited. He said, "Bessie, I found it, I found it!"

The next day Big Jim told Massa Henry that he had found the plant that he believed could cure him. Massa Henry wanted to start immediately drinking the tea from the plant but he told Big Jim he had to consult his doctor before using the plant. When Massa Henry told Dr. Dunn that Big Jim was going to use tea from a plant root to cure him, the doctor went berserk. He said, "Henry, stay away from those roots and herbs! That old stuff will kill you. Big Jim learned about that stuff from Uncle Charlie before he died. Uncle Charlie was a witch doctor in Africa before he was brought to South Carolina. They say Uncle Charlie messed up lots of slaves with that stuff. Henry, I'm telling you now, don't use that stuff! If the doctors here in Charleston can't cure you, then you know that stuff can't cure you either."

Massa Henry replied, "Dr. Dunn, I respect your advice but I am going to try it. I believe Big Jim can cure me with the tea from that plant root. I'm a dying man; I don't have much to lose anyway."

With Massa Henry's consent, Big Jim began doctoring on him in mid-November. Big Jim took the root from the plant and made a tea from it. He gave the tea to Massa Henry once in the morning and once at night. By Christmas Massa Henry was feeling better and had regained his appetite. Big Jim continued to give the tea to Massa Henry. By March of the next year, 1853, Massa Henry was cured of his mysterious illness. He was one happy man. His strength had returned, he no longer had fever and chills at night, and he no longer had that choking cough. He told Big Jim that he hadn't felt so good in over thirty years. The tea had completely revitalized his system. He was eighty-one but felt like a man in his fifty's.

Meanwhile, Big Jim was busy thinking about his future. He had cured Massa Henry, which meant that the plantation and all the slaves would not be sold to old, evil Mr. Travis. With Massa Henry alive and healthy and able to run the plantation, all the slaves on the plantation were now safe from the cruelty of Mr. Travis. However, Big Jim was still a slave and he didn't want to remain a slave. He wanted his freedom. He, therefore, began to plan his escape for May.

When Big Jim told Bessie about his planned escape, she was all for it. She said, "Big Jim, I know you miss your freedom and your family. You are doing right to try to escape. I wish I could be free. I heard a white man who came here to visit Massa Henry last year say that there may be a war between the North and the South one day, and if the North won, all the slaves would be set free. Isn't that something? I hope that day comes. Big Jim, I would love to be free."

Big Jim replied, "Bessie, I believe the war is going to come. There is much anger between the North and South over the issue of slavery."

One day in late April, Massa Henry told Bessie to tell Big Jim to come to his room; he had something to tell him. When Big Jim walked into Massa Henry's room, he saw a big smile on his face. Massa Henry said, "Big Jim, I am setting you free. You are too good a man to be a slave. You brought laughter into my sister Sue Ann's life over thirty years ago. Now you have cured me from the mysterious illness that I had. You are a credit to your race. I got my lawyer to make you some freedom papers so you can travel back to Pennsylvania on the stagecoach. They are on my desk over there. I've also bought you a new suit, a new pair of shoes, and a new hat to wear on your trip back home. You can leave Saturday on your trip back to Philadelphia."

When the stagecoach stopped at the Mills' plantation that Saturday morning to pick up Big Jim, everyone on the plantation was there to say good-bye. After telling everyone good-bye, Big Jim stepped up into the stagecoach. He was sharp as a tack, wearing a new hat, a new suit, and a new pair of shoes. In his hands were a bag and his freedom papers. He was headed up North once again to the "Promised Land."

ANALYSIS OF STORY

The story "The Legend of Big Jim" revolved around the life and times of the giant slave Big Jim. He was born free in Africa but was kidnapped at the age of nine, put on a slave ship, and brought to a Charleston, South Carolina slave market in 1807. He was purchased by a wealthy cotton planter named Henry Mills, who named him Jim. The boy, Jim, grew up to be a giant and became known as "Big Jim." His storytelling ability made him the slavemaster's favorite slave. When he successfully made Massa Henry's depressed sister laugh, his fame became widespread in the Charleston area. Big Jim became dissatisfied with slave life, thanks to encouragement from a rebellious slave named Abraham. In 1829 he, Abraham, and another slave named Turkey Man escaped up North to the free state of Pennsylvania. In Pennsylvania Big Jim married and became a successful farmer. In 1852 he was captured under a stipulation by slave catchers and brought back to Massa Henry, his old slavemaster in South Carolina. Big Jim cured the dying Massa Henry of a mysterious illness, which kept the slaves on the plantation from being sold to a cruel and abusive slavemaster named Mr. Travis. In the end, Massa Henry freed Big Jim and he left on a stagecoach bound for home in Pennsylvania.

This story gives a lesson to the reader. The lesson is stay alert, don't forget your history because you can end up repeating it. Big Jim tasted freedom, became complacent, went to sleep and forgot about his past (his stipulation), and ended up back in slavery. So, always stay alert, because if you don't, it can be to your detriment.

THE LEGEND OF BIG JIM

Big Jim was a giant slave who was
Born in Africa and raised down South
He could make you laugh
If you could open your mouth.

Big Jim's comic exploits made
Him a legend in his own time,
He was to comedy what
Age is to a good wine.

Big Jim was introduced to a woman who

Hadn't laughed in twenty years,
But when he told her a funny story she
Laughed so hard that she was in tears.

Big Jim was as strong
As a man could be
He could lift a bale of cotton
And break an oak tree.

Big Jim was daring and brave
He told Tom, man can't you see,
You have to take a risk
If you ever want to be free.

Big Jim was as big as a mountain
And as tall as a pine tree,
But on the dance floor
He was as nimble as a bee.

Big Jim became friends with Abraham and
Turkey Man, they formed a little band,
And they escaped up North
To the Promised Land.

On Mr. Coffin's farm in Pennsylvania
They had a big celebration
Observing their daring escape
From Massa Henry's plantation.

At a dance in Philadelphia Big Jim met the
Prettiest girl that he had ever seen in his life
With his great charm he captured her
Heart and made her his wife.

Big Jim was captured by slave
Catchers and reenslaved,
But when he cured his sick
Slavemaster everyone was amazed.

Big Jim's slavemaster said he was
Too good a man to be a slave,
So he set him free
For the rest of his days.

Big Jim got on the stagecoach
With his baggage in his hand
He was headed up North
To the Promised Land.

Robert L. Bradley, 12-16-97

STORY TWO

What Love Can Do

▼▼

IT WAS THE FALL OF 1966 WHEN BOBBIE HINES AND HIS BEST FRIEND
Chester Windgate entered Lewis College in New Orleans, Louisiana. Bobbie chose business administration as his major and accounting as his minor. Chester chose psychology as his major and history as his minor. Both young men had an enjoyable and exciting college life. In May of 1970 the two best friends graduated with honors from Lewis College.

A week after graduation the two best friends met at a restaurant to eat some good soul food and rap about their future. Chester said to Bobbie, "Man, my goal is to become a psychologist. I want to counsel and help people. I'm going to graduate school this fall to pursue a master's degree in psychology. What are your plans, Bobbie?"

Bobbie answered, "First, I'm going to marry my sweetheart Joan, and then I'm going up North to Milwaukee where my Uncle Dave lives and get myself a job."

Chester said, "Man, you are getting married mighty quick. I thought you were going to enjoy the single life some before you got

▼

married. Joan has blown your mind, man. She is an attractive woman and all that, but I didn't believe she could hook a player like you."

Bobbie replied, "Chester, I didn't believe I could get hooked either. But I am deeply in love with this fine, high-yellow girl. I'm going to marry her in August, and I would like for you to be my best man, please."

Chester said, "Bobbie, you are my best friend, man. You know I don't mind being your best man at the wedding. I hope you and Joan have a very successful marriage. I also hope you find a good job in Milwaukee. Next week, I'm going to Houston, Texas to work on a summer job, but I'll be back in New Orleans for your wedding in August."

The two best friends walked out of the restaurant, shook hands, and told each other good-bye until August 27, the date of the wedding.

As Chester walked to his car, he thought to himself, "Bobbie is my best friend but he has always had this problem with color. He is dark- skin himself but he likes only light-skinned black women; he has never dated a dark or brown-skin black woman to my knowledge. However, sisters come in different colors, yellow, brown, dark-brown, and dark. An attractive sister is an attractive sister regardless of color."

In August, Bobbie and Joan had a beautiful church wedding. Lots of friends and relatives attended the wedding. Joan's maid of honor was her sister; Bobbie's best man was his good friend Chester Windgate. After the wedding, Bobbie and Joan went to Milwaukee where Bobbie's uncle had an apartment waiting for them to live in.

With his good credentials, Bobbie soon found a job in Milwaukee. He was hired by the Sylvester Cheese Company. His wife found a job teaching in the public school system.

Bobbie proved to be a good worker at the Sylvester Cheese Company. He was hard working, likeable, and easy to train. His supervisor was impressed with his excellent work and when the fiscal year ended, he gave him an outstanding evaluation with a nice cash award. Bobbie Hines was very proud of his accomplishment and it whetted his appetite for more recognition. In 1973, after three years on the job, Bobbie applied for a supervisor position and, to his surprise, he beat out dozens of more experienced employees and got the position. Being selected supervisor made Bobbie very happy and proud. He was in such a good mood that he telephoned his best friend from his college days, Chester Windgate, and told him about his accomplishment. Chester congratulated him and told him he was happy for him.

Bobbie Hines continued to move up the ladder with the Sylvester Cheese Company. In 1975 he applied for a position as a branch manager and was selected to fill the position. In 1978 Bobbie was promoted to division manager. In 1980 he was selected over a large number of applicants to the position of department manager. This new position put him in charge of the Sylvester Cheese Company's production department, which comprised hundreds of workers. This new position also really boosted Bobbie's ego and some of his co-workers began to see arrogance in his behavior.

In 1981 Bobbie was feeling so good about himself that he decided to enroll part-time in graduate school to pursue a master's degree in business administration. He studied hard and by the spring of 1983 he had earned his M.B.A., which made him so proud.

After getting his M.B.A. degree, Bobbie began thinking seriously about his future with the Sylvester Cheese Company, and he came to the conclusion that he wanted to be the president of the company one day. Although he had a M.B.A. degree, he believed that wasn't quite good enough to get him to the position of president of the company. He felt that in order to move up higher in the company, he needed to change his appearance to a "crossover look" so management would feel more comfortable with him.

During the summer of 1983 Bobbie began to change his appearance; he wanted to look as "white" as possible. Feeling dissatisfied with his wooly hair, he went to a beauty salon and got himself a Luster curl. Feeling dissatisfied with his dark- skin, he purchased a skin-lightening cream and used it to lighten his skin. When he looked in the mirror, he still wasn't satisfied with his appearance. He felt it needed more enhancement. He, therefore, went to a surgeon and had his thick lips changed into thin ones. Still feeling dissatisfied with his appearance, he went back to the surgeon and had his flat nose changed into a straight one. After he had enhanced his appearance, Bobbie felt he looked more acceptable to the mainstream of society, and he was ready to compete with anyone for any position in the company.

In 1985 the position of vice-president of the Sylvester Cheese Company became vacant. When Bobbie Hines learned of the position vacancy, he felt that he was well- qualified for it. He had excellent writing and communication skills, he had leadership experience, he had a M.B.A. degree, and he possessed a "crossover look." However, there were other well-qualified people applying for the position too. The competition for the position was intense. It took the selection committee weeks to examine all the resumes and to interview the finalists for the position. Finally, the selection committee announced the person it had chosen for the position and the person was Bobbie Hines. His selection to the position of vice-president of the Sylvester Cheese Company caused lots of mixed emotions among the company's employees. Some employees thought Bobbie was well- qualified for the position, whereas others felt he had gotten the position by knowing the right people.

Being selected to the position of vice-president of the Sylvester Cheese Company had quite an effect on Bobbie Hines. It greatly inflated his ego and swelled his head to twice its size. One day he was overheard asking a man at the cheese plant who had accidentally stepped on his spit-shined shoes, "Mister, do you know who I am?"

The man replied, "No, I don't know who you are. Who are you?"

Bobbie said, "Don't you know, I'm Bobbie Hines, vice-president of the Sylvester Cheese Company. And from now on you had better watch where you are going."

Although Bobbie Hines had been very successful at the Sylvester Cheese Company, he hadn't fared as well with the blacks there. They saw him as selfish, arrogant, and insensitive to the plight of his people. One day during the summer of 1987, a community activist named Paul Scott had a candid conversation with Bobbie after playing a round of golf with him. Paul Scott said to Bobbie, "Man, I heard your relationship with blacks at the Sylvester Cheese Company leaves much to be desired. They say you are all for yourself. You don't try to use your high position to help other blacks advance their careers."

Paul's frank words surprised and irritated Bobbie. He responded angrily, "I'm not going to help those blacks where I work. They are lazy. They are always whining about racism and how the white man is holding them back. They need to work hard like I do, go back to school and take courses to make themselves more qualified, and quit using racism as an excuse for their lack of advancement on the job. If they do that, then they will get somewhere. But they refuse to do that. They just sit around and complain about how they are being discriminated against. They are jealous of my success. If they worked hard like me, they could be successful too. But they want something for nothing. I got mine and they have to get theirs."

Paul said, "Man, you are coming down on the 'brothers and sisters' at the cheese plant real hard, but you benefited from the 'brothers and sisters' who came before you. If it weren't for the civil rights movement that eliminated much discrimination in hiring, you never would have made vice-president of a white owned company. You didn't get where you are by yourself. You had help, but you don't want to help anyone else. That is being selfish."

The truth of Paul's words stung and angered Bobbie. He replied, "Excuse me, man, but who made me is me. I studied very hard to get my B.A. in business administration. I busted my behind to work my way up from a production worker to vice-president of the company. I even returned to school to get my M.B.A. degree. It was hard getting that M.B.A. I worked during the day and went to school at night. No one has given me anything. I've worked hard to get where I am."

Paul said, "Bobbie, I refuse to get into a heated argument with you about your relationship with the 'brothers and sisters' at your job, but don't get so high and mighty that you forget your roots. Remember these words of wisdom: 'Sometimes when you forget your past, your past has a way of catching up with you.' I hope you know what I mean."

Meanwhile, Bobbie Hines continued to work at the Sylvester Cheese Company and enjoy the good life. He had lots of money in the bank. He owned a flashy car, a Jaguar. He was a happy married man with two bright kids. His wife Joan was an elementary school principal. He lived in a nice home far out in the suburbs, having left the city of Milwaukee in 1983, the year he had received his M.B.A. degree. The reason he said he had moved away from the black community was to get away from drugs, crime and violence, and loud music.

In March of 1992 Bobbie Hines heard some news that really excited him. The news was Mr. Kurt von Eric, the president of the

Sylvester Cheese Company, had announced unexpectedly that he was retiring at the end of the year. He had recommended that Bobbie Hines replace him. However, a majority of the company's stockholders wanted the position to be filled competitively and they were allowed to have their way. A committee was formed to select a person to fill the position.

A large number of qualified people applied for the position. Bobbie Hines was one of them. He was very confident that he was going to get the position. He told some co-workers that he was the best man for the job, and he was going to get it. He boasted, " I'm the most qualified of all the applicants. I know the company in and out. I am forty-five years old and have twenty-two years with the company. And furthermore, I'm Bobbie Hines, vice-president of the company. I have a M.B.A. degree; I have excellent writing and communicating skills; I am a natural born leader; and I have a 'crossover look' to make the mainstream of society more comfortable with me. When I am selected for the position, I will be the company's first black president."

By September the selection committee had narrowed the large number of applicants down to two candidates, Bobbie Hines and John von Eric, the nephew of the retiring president. John von Eric was tall, handsome, and charismatic. He was also well educated but he lacked Bobbie Hines' many years of experience with the company, having only nine years.

In early October the selection committee gathered in the company's conference room to determine whom to choose for the position of president of the company, Bobbie Hines or John von Eric. When the selection committee members' votes were counted, Bobbie Hines held a slight edge in votes over John von Eric. As a result, it looked like Bobbie Hines was going to be the company's next president. However, when an old stockholder with a bald head got up and gave an impromptu speech, reminding the selection committee the importance of a president's image to the success of the company, his stirring words caused several committee members to change their votes in favor of John von Eric. In the final vote tally, John von Eric edged Bobbie Hines by two votes. He was, therefore, selected to fill the position of president of the Sylvester Cheese Company, replacing his Uncle Kurt von Eric.

Bobbie was devastated when he learned that he had not been selected to fill the position of president of the Sylvester Cheese Company. He couldn't believe he hadn't gotten the position. He said to some of his co-workers, "I know I was the most qualified person for the position, but I didn't get it. I was denied the position because I am black. It was an act of racism, plain and simple. I should have gotten that position. I'm going to get my lawyer and file a complaint against the company with the Equal Employment Opportunity Commission."

The more Bobbie thought about his situation, the more depressed he became. His wife Joan tried to console him but she couldn't. His Uncle Dave tried to console him but he couldn't either. No one could console Bobbie. As the days passed, he became more and more depressed over not being selected to fill the position of president. He eventually took a leave of absence from his job. One day he told Joan that he was so depressed that he felt like ending his life. The talk of suicide frightened Joan; she didn't know what to do. Suddenly it dawned on her that his best friend during his college days, Chester Windgate, might be able to help him. Chester was a person that Bobbie had always trusted and believed in. She, therefore, called Chester in Chicago and told him about Bobbie's depressed condition. Chester was saddened to hear about Bobbie's condition and told Joan he would drive from Chicago to Milwaukee to see him.

Joan was very happy that Chester was coming to help her husband Bobbie. She believed that if anyone could help him, he could. Chester was a brilliant clinical psychologist with a Ph.D. in psychology. He had a great understanding of psychology and how to apply it to help black people. He also had a great understanding of the effects of racism on the black mind. Chester and Bobbie had been friends since their high school days in Louisiana and had attended college together. Bobbie respected Chester's knowledge and believed in him. Although Bobbie hadn't seen Chester in three years, the two talked often on the telephone.

Within two hours of leaving Chicago, Chester arrived at the Hines' home in Milwaukee. He greeted each member of the Hines family very warmly. They were glad to see each other. Chester said to Bobbie, "Man, I am so happy to see you. This is 1992 and I haven't seen you since 1989. How are you feeling?"

Bobbie answered, "Man, I am not feeling well. I was denied a promotion to president of the Sylvester Cheese Company and it has devastated me. That was the one thing in life that I really wanted but I couldn't get it. Now, I have nothing to live for. I am thinking about ending it all."

Chester said, "Bobbie, don't say that. You have plenty to live for. You have a beautiful wife and two wonderful kids who love you. They would really miss you if you were gone! You have relatives and friends who love you and would miss you if you were gone. I love you like a brother and I would miss you so much if you were gone. God loves you and will help you overcome this depression if you ask Him to. Think about it; you have plenty to live for. Being president of a company is not the most important thing in the world. There are other more important things that you can do in life."

Bobbie replied, "Chester, you are right. I do have plenty to live for. Thanks, for coming to see about me. Your encouraging words have really lifted my spirits."

Chester said, "Bobbie, I am going to do everything in my power to help you overcome this depression. But in the meantime, I want you to begin attending Northside Baptist Church here in Milwaukee. The pastor of the church, Rev. Holmes, is a good friend of mine. He will be glad to have you as a member of his church."

Bobbie said, "Chester, I will do that."

While driving his car back home to Chicago, Chester was thinking about Bobbie's condition. He diagnosed him as suffering from depression, self-hate, and an inferiority complex. He knew Bobbie was in bad shape, but he believed he could help him overcome his problems. First, he had to help him overcome his depression, and then he would work on the other two problems later.

Chester, being a brilliant psychologist, was well aware of what had triggered Bobbie's depression. He understood that Bobbie's feelings of rejection and humiliation, after failing to get the position of president of the company, had brought on his depression. Bobbie had boasted to co-workers that he was certain to get the position, but when he failed to get it, his ego had suffered a terrible blow, causing him to feel rejected and humiliated. So rejected and humiliated, in fact, that he had talked about committing suicide.

Chester was also aware that Bobbie would need plenty of love and support from him, his family, and Northside Baptist Church in order to overcome his depressed state. Chester's aim was to use love and support to take Bobbie out of his depressed state of mind into a positive state of mind.

Bobbie joined Northside Baptist Church. He found the people at the little church to be warm, friendly, and down to earth. The services at the little church were lively and inspirational and Bobbie really enjoyed them. Sometimes his wife and kids attended the services with him. Bobbie felt loved, supported, and needed at the little church, which made him feel so good inside. Also the people at the little church accepted Bobbie for who he was, he didn't have to put on airs to try to impress them. As Bobbie continued to attend services at Northside Baptist Church, the better he felt. By June of 1993 Bobbie no longer talked about the Sylvester Cheese Company nor going back to it to work, instead he talked mostly about the people at Northside Baptist Church and how much he loved them.

One evening in early July, Chester Windgate telephoned his friend Bobbie Hines to see how he was doing. He said, "Hello, Bobbie, this is your friend Chester, calling you from Chicago. How are you feeling?"

Bobbie replied, "Man, I am feeling so good. In fact, I have never felt better in my life. I no longer think about being president of the Sylvester Cheese Company because it is no longer important to me. Also, I have completely recovered from my depression. I attribute my recovery from depression to all the love and support I have received; without it, I wouldn't have been able to recover from my depression. Chester, I love you, my family, and Northside Baptist Church so very much. You all stuck by me in a time of trouble."

Chester was so amazed at what Bobbie said that he was speechless. He had never heard him talk like that before. Proud and self-conceited Bobbie Hines being humble, thankful, and full of love, it was a beautiful thing to hear. Fighting back his emotions, Chester finally said, "Bobbie, I am so happy that you have recovered from your depression. What are your plans for the future? Are you going back to work at the Sylvester Cheese Company?"

Bobbie answered, "Chester, at the present time I don't know what my future plans are. But I know for sure, I'm not going back to work at the Sylvester Cheese Company."

Now that he had helped Bobbie to overcome his depression,

Chester wanted to also help him overcome his self-hate and inferiority complex. Chester had known for a long time that Bobbie was ashamed of his blackness and wanted to escape from it. Also, Chester understood that Bobbie's "crossover look" was a futile attempt to escape his blackness.

Chester was not only a brilliant psychologist but also a good historian. He knew the complete history of black people, from their glorious past to the present. His aim was to use black history to help Bobbie to overcome his self-hate and inferiority complex.

In August, Chester came to Milwaukee to visit Bobbie and his family. When he got ready to leave, he told Bobbie that he had some black history books for him to read. Bobbie reluctantly took the books from Chester and told him he would read them.

Bobbie's knowledge of black history was limited. He had always disliked it. He had taken the black history books from Chester only because he didn't want to hurt his feelings. Bobbie saw no significance in reading black history. Either it made him feel lots of pain, or it made him feel ashamed. To Bobbie, black history was only about Africa and slavery, two subjects he detested. He had been ashamed of Africa ever since he had watched the picture, Tarzan, on television as a kid back in the early 1960s. The Africans on Tarzan had been so stupid, cowardly, and primitive that he had felt humiliated by their negative image. And ever since then he hadn't wanted anything to do with Africa. Reading about the cruelty that his forefathers had endured during slavery had always made him feel sad. In short, because of the negativity associated with black history, Bobbie had never wanted to read about it.

For weeks Bobbie ignored the black history books that Chester had brought for him to read; finally one day in early November he picked up one of the books and decided to read it. The book was entitled "Egypt Revisited," edited by a scholar named Ivan Van

Sertima. After reading the book, Bobbie was so shocked that he sat on his sofa and trembled. He had never read anything like it before. The well-documented book had pointed out that ancient Egypt, the greatest civilization in antiquity, was created by black people. Bobbie found it hard to believe that blacks had once made extraordinary cultural achievements and had once built architectural wonders such as colossal pyramids, dazzling sphinxes, and huge temples. But the many pictures in the book showing ancient Egyptians with unmistakable Negroid features convinced Bobbie that the ancient Egyptians had been a black people.

The reading of this amazing book created a desire in Bobbie to read the other books about black history that Chester had left. After reading these books, Bobbie learned many interesting things about Africa that he didn't know. He learned that in addition to Egypt, there were other cultures in Africa that had a high degree of achievement, including the Swahili culture along the coast of East Africa during the Middle Ages; the West African culture that produced the medieval empires of Ghana, Mali, and Songhay; and, of course, the culture of the ancient African state of Ethiopia. He also learned that there was African resistance to the slave trade, and the most famous ruler to resist was a woman named Queen Nzinga. Bobbie had never known that there had been African resistance to the slave trade, he had only known about the Africans that sold other Africans.

The reading of the black history books had turned on a light in Bobbie's mind and he was hungry for more knowledge. He telephoned Chester and told him to bring him some books about the history of blacks in America. And, of course, Chester brought them for him to read. After reading the books on African-American history, Bobbie was very enlightened. He had always thought that blacks had been weak and fragile during slavery, but he learned that they had showed much strength and resiliency during slavery, having been able to survive the most inhumane slavery known to man. He had always thought that blacks had been docile and obedient during slavery, but he learned that they had also run away and rebelled. In addition, he learned that blacks had made a big contribution to the greatness of American culture, including roles other than as slaves and servants, such as soldiers, leaders, inventors, educators, scientists, and scholars.

By July of 1994 Bobbie had read many books about black history and the knowledge he had gained had effected him tremendously. His whole attitude about Africa and his blackness had changed completely. He was no longer ashamed of Africa or to be of African descent. He had overcome his self-hate and inferiority complex.

One evening Bobbie called his friend Chester and asked him to bring him some more black history books to read. Chester said to Bobbie, "Man, you must really enjoy reading those black history books!"

Bobbie replied, "Man, I sure do. The books you have loaned me approach black history from a more positive perspective, in contrast to the general history books that show black history in a negative light. That is why I enjoy your books. They discuss achievements, heroes, and the strengths of black people instead of just a negative story."

Chester said, "Bobbie, it is so wonderful that you now enjoy reading about black history. Has reading about black history affected you in any way?"

Bobbie said, "Yes, reading about black history has had a big affect on me. It has changed how I perceive Africa and myself. I am no longer ashamed of Africa or my blackness. I have developed self-love. It is such a wonderful feeling to have self-love. I am also no longer ashamed to be associated with the black community."

Chester couldn't believe what he was hearing. It sounded so

beautiful to hear him talk about self-love. He had now helped Bobbie to overcome his self-hatred and inferiority complex. Chester said, "Man, I am glad that you have changed your attitude about Africa, yourself, and the black community. I'm going to bring you some more black history books to read. One of these books is very special. It is called 'The Mis-education of the Negro,' written by the late African-American historian Carter G. Woodson. I want you to read it first. I believe you will enjoy it. I will bring the books to you this Saturday. Good-bye, my brother."

Bobbie could hardly wait for Saturday to come. He was anxious to read the book "The Mis-education of the Negro." Finally Saturday came and Chester brought him the black history books that he had promised him, including the book "The Mis-education of the Negro." As soon as Chester left his house, Bobbie picked up the book and began reading it. He found the book to be enjoyable, the gospel truth, and relevant, even though it had been first published in 1933. The book pointed out that blacks had been mis-educated. They had been taught how to serve and follow others rather than how to think and do for themselves. Also, many so-called educated blacks had not been taught how to apply what they had learned to uplift their people.

Bobbie thought to himself, "I thought I was educated but the truth is I have been mis-educated. My education lacked positive black history and that is one of the reasons why I manifested self-hate and an inferiority complex. However, thanks to my friend Chester, I have overcome it. I also was taught to serve others and that is the reason why I have never thought about creating my own job, even though I have a M.B.A. degree."

Suddenly it dawned on Bobbie that he should create his own job, now that he no longer worked for the Sylvester Cheese Company. He thought about what kind of job could he create. As he continued to think, the idea of being a businessman popped into his mind. He felt he was well qualified to be a businessman. He had two degrees in business administration and he had nineteen years of management experience. After analyzing his qualifications, Bobbie concluded that he would be a businessman. As a businessman, he would not only create his own job but he would also create jobs for others.

When Bobbie looked at the cover of the book "The Mis-education of the Negro," he thought to himself, "Why haven't more African-Americans used this book to help solve the problems of the black community? Don't they realize that solutions to problems in our community are right here in this book. Well, if many blacks haven't used it, I'm sure going to use it."

Bobbie's aim was to establish businesses in the black community, which would in turn create jobs. His new self-love had inspired him to want to uplift the black community; he no longer wanted to disassociate himself from it. Bobbie felt that he was now the new Bobbie Hines, who was unselfish, caring, and loving. The old Bobbie Hines, who was selfish, arrogant, and self-conceited, had been put to rest when he quit the Sylvester Cheese Company. Bobbie knew that he couldn't change how he had mistreated the "brothers and sisters" at the Sylvester Cheese Company, but he would try to compensate for it by doing his best to help the unemployed in the black community.

Bobbie was very excited when he told his wife Joan about his plan to open businesses in the black community. She told him that it was a good idea and she believed it would be successful. Bobbie also told his friend Chester and his pastor Rev. Holmes about his plan to open businesses in the black community to create jobs. They both thought it was a good idea and told him that they would help him any way that they could.

One morning, while eating breakfast, Bobbie's mind shifted to the subject of businesses. He had observed black businesses and believed that two of the reasons they failed were because their prices were too high and their workers disrespectful attitude toward customers. Bobbie planned to avoid those weaknesses when he became a businessman.

After thinking it over carefully, Bobbie decided to go into the restaurant and dry cleaning business. He was an excellent cook, having learned how to cook from his mother when he was a kid down in Louisiana. She had given him some of her secrets to cooking delicious fish, chicken, red beans and rice, and other foods. His grandparents on his father's side had owned a dry cleaning business, and he had worked in it as a teenager.

In December, Bobbie decided that he was going to open a restaurant in the next year. He set the opening date for the spring of 1995.

Bobbie was bubbling over with enthusiasm when he opened his Bayou Restaurant in North Milwaukee in March of 1995. A large crowd was there, including most of the members from his church. The customers found his food delicious, his prices very competitive, his workers very courteous, and his restaurant clean and attractive. As the months passed customers continued to come to his restaurant in large numbers to eat his delicious, down home style food: chicken, fish, red beans and rice, shrimp, and other delicacies. By December Bobbie was doing so well financially that he decided to open another Bayou Restaurant. He opened it in April of 1996. Like the other Bayou Restaurant, this one was also a financial success. In July of 1997 Bobbie opened a dry cleaning business which attracted lots of customers because of its competitive prices.

By September of 1999 Bobbie had three Bayou restaurants and two dry cleaning businesses in operation in the African-American community, and each one was making money. These businesses had created jobs in the black community. Customers were attracted to Bobbie's businesses because they got good service and competitive prices. Even some of Bobbie's old co-workers from the Sylvester Cheese Company patronized his businesses, including some whites who ate at his restaurants.

In December of 1999 Bobbie was honored by a civic group that selected him minority businessman of the year in Milwaukee. This honor made him feel so proud. He was very happy to be recognized for his good work in the black community where he was creating jobs and helping the poor.

On New Year's Day, 2000, Bobbie was helping his wife prepare dinner, when he said, "Joan, I have been working very hard since I opened the first Bayou Restaurant in March of 1995 and I need a long vacation."

Joan replied, "Bobbie, where are you thinking about going?"

Bobbie said, "Joan, I want to take a long vacation in Africa. I want to visit the continent where our ancestors came from."

Joan replied, "What? You want to visit Africa? Why do you want to go to Africa?"

Bobbie said, "I have been doing lots of reading about Africa's glorious past and there are some things there that I want to see. I especially want to see two architectural wonders that my ancestors built: the Great Pyramids in Egypt and Great Zimbabwe, the ruins of a huge stone city, hundreds of years old, located in the present-day nation of Zimbabwe."

Joan replied, "Well, Bobbie, I hope you enjoy your vacation in Africa."

Bobbie said, "Not so fast, I want you and the kids to go with me."

Joan replied, "Bobbie, you have to be kidding. There is nothing in Africa that I want to see."

Bobbie said, "Joan, don't say that. Africa has a very negative image in the eyes of the world, but there are some positive things that are going on there. You will enjoy Africa if you go there."

Joan replied, "All right, Bobbie, the kids and I will go with you to Africa but we better enjoy ourselves there."

Bobbie said, "You all will enjoy yourselves in Africa, you will see."

In February, Bobbie and his family began planning their trip to Africa. They decided to spend the whole summer of 2000 touring Africa, first visiting the Great Pyramids in Egypt, then moving down the East Coast of Africa to Southern Africa to see the ruins of Great Zimbabwe, then pushing on up the West Coast of Africa to Ghana.

Meanwhile, in March on a cold day at a restaurant in North Milwaukee, a little group was eating supper at a table and rapping. The men and women in this little group were of different faiths and philosophies but they all got along well together. It was amazing how they were able to overcome their differences and find common ground. Of course, they had their share of heated arguments but they knew how to disagree with each other without falling out. They attributed their ability to get along with each other to their love and respect for each other. As the members of this little group continued to rap, one member, Brother Armstrong, a community activist, asked the question, "Did anyone read the article in the newspaper last week about businessman Bobbie Hines?"

Some in the little group had read the article in the newspaper and others hadn't. Brother Ahmed, Brother Irons, Sister Nesbitt, and Sister White had read the article in the newspaper about Bobbie Hines, most of the others in the little group hadn't.

Speaking to those who hadn't read the article, Brother Armstrong said, "The article about businessman Bobbie Hines was very interesting. Within a short period of time he has become a very successful businessman. He was chosen minority businessman of the year in Milwaukee for 1999."

Brother Ahmed, a devout Muslim, said to Brother Armstrong, "I enjoyed the article about businessman Bobbie Hines but I don't believe I know him."

Brother Armstrong replied, "Yes, you do know him, Brother Ahmed. He used to come into this restaurant back in the 1980s and eat here. He was the brother who had the 'crossover look'— Luster Curl, bleached skin, and surgery on his nose and lips. While eating his food, he would boast about his good job at the Sylvester Cheese Company and his big bank account. He would also put the 'brothers and sisters' down who worked with him. He would say that they were lazy and were always whining about racism, and he wasn't going to help them advance their careers."

Brother Ahmed said, "Yes, I do remember that brother now. He was trying to escape from his blackness. He was one confused brother. But I am very happy that he has changed and is now working in the African-American community, trying to uplift his people."

Brother Armstrong replied, "Yes, that brother who used to come in here and talk all that negative talk about the black community is businessman Bobbie Hines. Isn't that something? However, he has changed. He now offers the black community help and encouragement, instead of just criticism. I am so proud of him. He is trying to create jobs for the unemployed in our community."

Sister Nesbitt, a bible toting Christian, entered the conversation, she said, "Bobbie Hines is a member of my church, Northside Baptist. We at Northside Baptist love him. He is caring, loving, and so unselfish. But when he first came to our church, he was suffering from depression and he was in bad shape. But we all prayed for him and God has brought him out of that depressed state. Yes, he has really changed. The old Bobbie Hines was selfish, self-hating, and arrogant. The new Bobbie Hines is humble, very unselfish, and is filled with love for everyone regardless of color. He is trying to uplift our community. He has five businesses in our community and has created jobs for our unemployed youth. I am so proud of him."

Brother Irons, a self-proclaimed black leader, entered the conversation. He said, "Bobbie Hines is doing the right thing by trying to empower the black community economically. We as a people are about 13 percent of the United States population but we own just about 2 percent of the businesses in the United States. We also earn over $400 billion a year as a people but very little if it is spent with black businesses. We as a people are mostly consumers; we are not sellers of goods and manufacturers of goods. That is the reason why so many of us live in poverty, we don't let our money work for us. Bobbie Hines is trying to help us keep some of our money in our community so it can work for us. I am so proud of him. We need more people in our community like him."

Sister White, a caring and very outspoken woman, entered the conversation. She said, "I am so proud of Bobbie Hines for trying to uplift our community. He deserves to be recognized because so many blacks, once they become successful, refuse to contribute to the very community that helped them to get where they are. Bobbie Hines was once a part of the problem but now he is a part of the solution."

Brother Ahmed reentered the conversation. He said, "I am proud of Brother Bobbie Hines too. He is practicing do for self. We as a people shouldn't look for others to do for us what we should be doing for ourselves."

Brother Armstrong said to the little group, "Guess what, brothers and sisters? The newspaper article also said that Bobbie Hines is planning to visit Africa this summer. Isn't that something?"

When he heard what Brother Armstrong said, Brother Sulu, a member of the little group who was from South Africa, almost fell out of his seat. But he quickly regained his balance. He then said with a smile, "Come on Brother Armstrong, you are kidding. Brother Bobbie Hines is planning to visit Africa. That is really something! However, I believe he will enjoy his trip to Africa. I am glad that he wants to visit the home of his ancestors. That's wonderful."

Brother Armstrong said, " Yes, Brother Sulu, the newspaper says that Bobbie Hines plans to visit Africa this summer. I hope he enjoys his trip."

Meanwhile, it was June 1, 2000. Bobbie Hines and his family were at the Milwaukee airport, in a few minutes they would be boarding the airplane to begin their trip to Africa. Bobbie said to his wife and kids, "Well, in a matter of minutes, we will be in the air, beginning our trip to Africa. I am so excited! When we get back home to Milwaukee, I plan to expand my businesses in the African-American community so I can create more jobs for the unemployed."

ANALYSIS OF STORY

The story "What Love Can Do" illustrates the power of love. Through the power of love Bobbie Hines overcame his depression, his self-hate, and inferiority complex.

Bobbie Hines falsely believed that he could escape his blackness. He changed his appearance to a new "crossover look," which he thought would make him more acceptable to the mainstream of society and would also improve his chances to move up to the position of president of the Sylvester Cheese Company. However, when he failed to be selected to the position of president of the company, he was so devastated that he went into a state of depression. But through love and support from his family, best friend, and church, he eventually overcame his depression.

Because he lacked self-love, Bobbie suffered from self-hate and an inferiority complex. However, through the reading of black history books that showed positive things about black people such as heroes, contributions, and achievements, Bobbie Hines became comfortable with his blackness and developed self-love. This new self-love changed Bobbie into a new person. He was no longer ashamed of Africa and wanted to go there to visit. He was no longer ashamed of being associated with the black community and wanted to help uplift it. He was also no longer ashamed of his blackness. In short, by developing self-love, Bobbie was able to overcome his self-hate and inferiority complex.

Love is a powerful emotion. It can work miracles. It helped Bobbie Hines to overcome his depression, his self-hate, and his inferiority complex.

This story gives an important lesson to the reader. The lesson is you can't escape from the way God made you. If you do try to escape, you are deluding yourself, because you can't be what you are not. So, you may as well be comfortable with the way God made you.

They All Came Together
to Uplift the Community

▼▼▼

DURING THE 1950S AND 1960S, LARGE NUMBERS OF BLACK LABORERS IN northeastern Arkansas were effected by the mechanization and sophistication of agriculture. Mechanical cotton pickers replaced their hand picking of cotton in the cotton fields. Weed killers replaced their hoe cultivation of cotton and soybean crops. Replaced by an increasing mechanization and sophistication of agriculture, many blacks left the plantations and towns of northeastern Arkansas to find employment up North. They left the northeastern Arkansas towns of Blytheville, Osceola, Luxora, Wilson, and Joiner to find employment in northern cities such as St. Louis, Chicago, Milwaukee, and Detroit.

Two of the people who left northeastern Arkansas to live in a northern city were Willie Spencer and his wife, Nora. In 1961 they left the town of River City, Arkansas and relocated in Detroit, Michigan. Within a month after arriving in Detroit, they both found jobs working at a factory that made auto parts. They both liked Detroit and decided to remain there and raise a family. In 1963 their first child was born; it was a boy. In 1966 they were blessed with a pair of twin girls. By 1971 the hardworking and thrifty couple had a nice home, money in the bank, and was doing well. In 1974 Willie was promoted to a first level supervisor at the auto parts plant. In 1981 Nora was also promoted to a first level supervisor position there. Throughout the remainder of the 1980s, Willie and Nora continued to work at the auto parts plant. In 1991 they both had thirty years of service at the plant and were talking about retirement. In June of 1994 Willie and Nora retired from their jobs at the auto parts plant with thirty-three years of service each.

One day in early July, Willie and Nora were barbecuing in their back yard when Willie said to Nora, "Honey, guess what? I've been thinking about us leaving Detroit and going back home to Arkansas to live, now that we have retired."

Nora replied, "Willie, I'm sorry but I don't want to live in River City, Arkansas again. We haven't lived there since 1961! It will be too much of an adjustment for me to live there again."

Willie said, "Nora, River City is no longer the little town we lived in thirty-three years ago. It has grown larger and has more to offer now. You saw how much it has grown when we were down there two years ago."

Nora replied, "Yes, I am aware that it has grown but I will still have problems adjusting to it. I have become used to living in a big city instead of a big town. And furthermore, if I leave Detroit I will miss our kids and all of our friends. Also, the kids are married and have jobs, and you know they are not going to relocate down South."

Willie said, "I will miss our friends too, and I will definitely miss our kids and grandchildren. But we can always come back to Detroit and visit them! I am just tired of living in a big city with all of its hustle and bustle. You know I'm a country boy; I now want to live in the quieter environment of northeastern Arkansas. Also, I am tired of the large amounts of snow and ice we get here in Detroit during the winter. Down South we don't get as much. I believe a change in climate will be better for my health; I'm not a spring chicken anymore. You know, I'll be sixty-one years old in September."

Nora replied, "Willie, I am still undecided about moving back to Arkansas. It has been so long since we last lived there. Give me a couple of weeks to think it over, then I'll give you a yes or no."

Nora thought long and hard for two weeks about moving back to Arkansas with Willie. Finally, she agreed to move back to Arkansas with Willie. His health was the determining factor in her decision. She believed the warmer climate down South would be better for his health.

When Nora told Willie that she would move back to River City, Arkansas with him, he became very excited. So excited, in fact, that he talked about the good times they had had down in Arkansas during their courting days back in the 1950s. Then he danced old dances and sang old songs from the late 50s and early 60s. Nora looked at him, shook her head, and burst out laughing.

After thinking it over carefully, Willie and Nora decided to move back to Arkansas in the coming year, 1995. But first they had to go to River City, Arkansas and find themselves a house to buy.

In April of 1995 Willie and Nora moved back to River City. They received a warm welcome from relatives, old friends, and old schoolmates. Some old friends and schoolmates hadn't seen them in thirty-four years and were very happy to see them.

Willie and Nora found that the town of River City had changed a lot since 1961. It had grown much larger and had more things to offer its residents. Segregation was gone; there were no more white and colored signs. Some middle class blacks had left the south side of town for the suburb of Cypress Gardens. Also the Southside or black section of town was now plagued by drugs, crime and violence, and high rates of unemployment, problems it didn't have when Willie and Nora lived there.

One day in late May, Willie visited his cousin Alice Brown whom he hadn't seen in nearly ten years. She was glad that he had stopped by to visit her. She was a wealthy beautician and a faithful churchgoer. To everyone in the community she was known as Sister Brown. For hours she and Willie laughed and talked about old times. Eventually, the subject switched to religion. She told Willie that she attended church every Sunday and had been doing so since she was a kid. Willie told her that he had rarely gone to church when he lived in Detroit, instead he had been into partying and having a good time. Sister Brown told him she wasn't trying to meddle in his business, but she thought he should begin thinking about joining a church so he could save his soul. Willie thanked her for her concern but told her he had already been talking to his wife Nora about joining a church.

Sister Brown thought for awhile, then she asked, "Willie, have you and Nora been looking for a church home since you all moved back to River City?"

Willie replied, "Yes, we have but we haven't found the right one yet."

Sister Brown said, "Well, you all don't have to look any longer. Come visit my church, Faith Missionary Baptist. I believe you and Nora will like it. In my opinion it is one of the best churches in town. It has over 800 members, but it is warm and friendly like a small country church. The pastor of Faith Missionary Baptist Church is Rev. Moses Wright, one preaching and singing man. Our assistant pastor is Rev. Harold Mays. He is also a good preacher. Our two pastors work well together and get along like brothers. My church, Faith Missionary Baptist, will be glad to have you and Nora as members."

Willie replied, "Nora and I will come to visit your church this Sunday, Alice. From your description of it, Faith Missionary Baptist Church is the type of church we want to join."

When Sunday arrived, Willie and Nora visited Sister Brown's church. They enjoyed its service and found it to be as warm and friendly as Sister Brown had described it. The next Sunday they returned to Faith Missionary Baptist Church and joined it. Pastor Wright was glad to have them as members and welcomed them with open arms. As they continued to attend services at Faith Missionary Baptist Church, they became more and more a part of it. By the spring of 1996, they had become so much a part of Faith Missionary Baptist Church that they felt like they had been attending it all of their lives. They had come to love this peaceful and warm church.

Willie and Nora were observing Faith Missionary Baptist Church from the surface instead of from beneath the surface. From the surface everything looked so peaceful and calm, but looking beneath the surface, things were not as peaceful and calm as they appeared. Trouble was brewing between Pastor Wright and Rev. Mays, his assistant. In a deacons' meeting, the two ministers had had a heated argument over Pastor Wright's lack of leadership in the black community. But the argument had been broken up by Brother Sanford, the church's oldest deacon.

After their argument, Pastor Wright and Rev. Mays agreed to meet in private at Brother Sanford's home to try to resolve their differences. At the meeting, Rev. Mays began the discussion. He said to Pastor Wright, "My dear brother, I am not trying to run your life, I just want to let you know that I am dissatisfied with your lack of leadership in the black community. The black community here in River City has problems such as crime and violence, drugs, and high unemployment, and you aren't doing anything to try to solve them. I feel you need to begin providing the black community with some strong leadership. You are more than qualified to do this. You are well-educated, you are a powerful orator, you have good leadership and fund-raising skills, and you have excellent social skills."

Pastor Wright replied, "Rev. Mays, I am most certainly aware of the pressing problems facing the black community here in River City, but I don't believe it is my job to try to solve them. It is the job of our elected officials and the business community here in River City to try to solve these problems. My job is to be the pastor of Faith Missionary Baptist Church. I am doing my job when I am leading this church. In fact, I believe I am a very good pastor. If any member of my church needs my help, he or she can call me day or night, and I will help him or her."

Rev. Mays said, "Come on Pastor Wright, wake up! You have the credentials to be more than just a church leader. You have the credentials to also be a community leader. You have good leadership ability, charm, and charisma. You are also the pastor of the largest and most prestigious church in the black community. When you speak, people listen. I believe you should work in the community as well as in the church. Remember, Jesus Christ worked among the people—feeding the hungry, healing the sick, and giving hope to the hopeless. Dr. King came down from the pulpit, went out into the streets, and helped to change things in this nation. Pastor Wright, you have the potential to change things here in River City. I hope you will do it."

Pastor Wright replied, "Well, don't get me wrong but I am a church leader, not a community leader. I am the Rev. Moses Wright, pastor of Faith Missionary Baptist Church. My job is to be the leader of this church. I've been leading this church for twenty years and I'm going to keep on doing what I've been doing."

Rev. Mays said, "I am sorry Pastor Wright but I can't continue to follow a man who refuses to climb down from the pulpit and go out into the community and work."

Pastor Wright replied, "Well, Rev. Mays, you do what you have to do, and I'm going to do what I have to do."

Rev. Mays said, "Pastor Wright, I believe I am going to have to do that."

Two weeks after his meeting with Pastor Wright, Rev. Mays announced to Faith Missionary Baptist Church that he was going to leave and start his own church. His announcement stunned the members of the church. They couldn't believe what they were hearing. They were left asking the question, what had happened between Pastor Wright and Rev. Mays?

At a special church meeting, Rev. Mays told the members of Faith Missionary Baptist Church the reason why he was leaving. He said to them, "Brothers and sisters, I am leaving to start another church, because I am dissatisfied with Pastor Wright's lack of leadership in uplifting the black community, and I can no longer follow it. My goal is to build my own church and use it as a base to help uplift the black community."

After learning why Rev. Mays was leaving, half of Faith Missionary Baptist Church decided to go with him, including deacons, mothers, choir members, and bench members. The split was so severe that it divided families, relatives, and friends. Brother Sanford, the church's oldest deacon, decided to remain with Pastor Wright, whereas his wife decided to leave with Rev. Mays. Willie decided to leave with Rev. Mays, whereas Nora decided to remain with Pastor Wright. Sister Brown, of course, decided to remain with her beloved minister, Pastor Wright.

The split of Faith Missionary Baptist Church shocked the black community of River City. People couldn't believe that the peaceful and friendly church had split up.

The split of Faith Missionary Baptist Church also generated much talk among residents of the black community in River City. They wanted to know what had caused Faith Missionary Baptist Church, a symbol of pride in the black community, to split up. They wanted to know why two ministers who had gotten along like brothers for years, were now unable to settle their differences.

As the residents of the black community continued to talk about the split up of Faith Missionary Baptist Church, answers to their questions began to become known. They learned what had caused the church to split up. They also learned why the two ministers were unable to settle their differences.

Among the people in the black community who talked about the church split up were three friends: Harry, the hustler; Walter, the wino; and Phyliss, the prostitute. One night while riding around in Harry's car, the three discussed the church split up. Harry, the hustler, asked Walter, the wino, "Walter, man, have you heard about the split up of Pastor Wright's church?"

Walter, the wino, answered, "Harry, man, you know I've heard about the split up of Pastor Wright's church. Everyone in town is talking about it! They say Rev. Mays just walked away from Pastor Wright and took about half of the church with him. It's too bad that the two preachers couldn't settle their differences. My cousin, who belongs to Faith Missionary Baptist Church, told me that Rev. Mays left because he and Pastor Wright didn't see eye to eye about helping the black community. Rev. Mays wanted Pastor Wright to become more involved in uplifting the Southside but he refused."

Harry, the hustler, said, "Walter, man, I've heard some things about Pastor Wright and Rev. Mays myself. I heard Pastor Wright will not help you unless you belong to his church. On the other hand, I heard Rev. Mays is different. They say he will help anyone if he can regardless of whether he or she belongs to a church. You know, last year he helped to stop the gangs from fighting each other. Rev. Mays is my kind of man."

Phyliss, the prostitute, entered the conversation. She said, "Walter, I thought those church people at Faith Missionary Baptist Church had it together too, but evidently they don't. Maybe one day they will get back together. You know, they're suppose to be setting an example for people like us."

Harry, Walter, and Phyliss were good friends, and they looked out for each other. They often hung out together at the corner of 28th St. and Monroe Ave. on the Southside of River City. Harry, the hustler, decked-out in a flashy suit and with a briefcase in his hand, would stand on the corner and sell stolen jewelry and drugs to his customers. Walter, the wino, with his dark-colored eyeglasses and ragged clothes, would stand on the corner and beg passersby for money to buy wine. Phyliss, the prostitute, with her fine self, would stand on the corner and sell her body to her customers.

One evening while standing at the corner of 28th St. and Monroe Ave., Harry, Walter, and Phyllis discussed their past. Phyllis asked Harry, "How long have you been hanging out on this corner selling hot items and drugs?"

Harry chuckled and replied, "Phyllis, I've been hanging out on this corner selling hot items and drugs for ten years. However, I've been hustling since I was a teenager. It's a long story but I will tell you some of it. When I was thirteen years old, my father deserted me, my mother, and my twelve brothers and sisters. My mother had a difficult time supporting us without him. I was always hungry and I had to wear secondhand clothes. To get food and nice clothes, I began stealing. After a while, I got good at it. When I was sixteen years old, I dropped out of high school and began hustling for a living. I sold stolen items and drugs, I did a little pimping, and I gambled with loaded dice. My hustling life eventually landed me in the state pen here in Arkansas. I was released from prison in 1986. When I came back to River City, I looked for a job but no one would hire me. So, I began hustling again for a living. Yes, Phyllis, I've been on this corner since 1986, ten years."

Walter said to Harry and Phyllis, "It's my turn to tell my story. I'm going to tell you all how I became a wino. In high school in Little Rock I was an outstanding basketball player. I made all-state and all-American my senior year. My aspiration was to become a pro basketball player. After graduating from high school, I left Little Rock and went away to college on a basketball scholarship. During my sophomore year in college I was averaging 30 points a game when I got kicked off the team for using drugs. That incident devastated me. I didn't know what to do after having been kicked off the basketball team. Instead of trying to play for another college or trying out for a pro team, I just gave up and slowly fell apart. Then, I started drinking wine to cope with my depression. Eventually, I became a wino, drinking wine everyday to escape the pain of my shattered dream of being a pro basketball player. In 1988 I left Little Rock and moved here to River City to live with my brother. In 1990 I began hanging out on this corner to beg passersby for money to buy wine. I've been on this corner for six years."

Phyllis said to Harry and Walter, "It's my turn to tell my story. I'm going to tell you all how I became a prostitute. When I was fifteen years old in high school, I fell in love with a twenty-two year old guy named Marlon Webber. He was a smooth talker, and he talked me into dropping out of high school and going to live with him. We stayed together for five years, and then he left me for another woman. I was devastated because I was so much in love with him. After losing him, I just fell apart and drifted into prostitution. In this prostitution business, I get paid for my love, and I don't get my feelings involved in it. It is just a business transaction and I don't have to worry about falling in love and getting hurt. Losing Marlon was such a blow to me that I don't know if I can ever love another man. I've been on this corner since 1991, five years."

The months passed quickly and it was now June of 1997, over a year since the split up of Faith Missionary Baptist Church, yet there had been no talk of reunification. Rev. Mays and Pastor Wright were still not talking to each other. They hadn't talked to each other since the church split up. Rev. Mays and his group of church members had service every Sunday in a school auditorium, but planned to build a church next spring and name it New Faith Missionary Baptist Church. On the other hand, Pastor Wright and his group of church members were still having service every Sunday at the old church.

One Friday evening in July, after some soul-searching, Rev. Mays decided to telephone Pastor Wright to see how he was doing. He called Pastor Wright and said, "Hello, Pastor Wright, my dear brother, how have you been doing?"

A surprised Pastor Wright replied, "I have been doing okay, Rev. Mays. I hope you have been doing okay, too."

Rev. Mays said, "My dear brother, I am asking you to forgive me for being so critical of your lack of leadership in the black community, and for splitting up Faith Missionary Baptist Church. Please don't hold anything in your heart against me. You know why I left."

Pastor Wright replied, "Rev. Mays, I have already forgiven you. I know why you left."

Rev. Mays said, "Pastor Wright, my dear brother, I still love you and I still love Faith Missionary Baptist Church. You all pray for me. I left the church because I want to work to uplift the black community, and it wasn't headed in that direction."

Pastor Wright replied, "Rev. Mays, I love you too and the church members who left with you. I understand why you left, and if you ever want to come back to Faith Missionary Baptist Church, you are welcome. It is so wonderful to hear your voice again. Goodbye."

Following the conversation, Pastor Wright thought to himself, "My lack of leadership in the black community caused Rev. Mays and half of the church to leave me. But trying to uplift the black community is a big challenge. I don't know whether to accept this big challenge or not."

Pastor Wright was unable to make a decision. He decided to turn the decision over into God's hands and let God guide him in the right direction. He then prayed and went to sleep.

When Pastor Wright woke up the next morning, he was very excited. He said to his wife, "Baby, guess what? Last night I had the most beautiful dream of my life. In my dream, I saw a revitalized black community here on the Southside, and it was a magnificent sight. There were thriving black businesses that had created lots of new jobs. There were nice rebuilt houses and apartments that had replaced old boarded-up houses and apartments. There was a new spirit of hope here on the Southside. There was a new spirit of striving for excellence here on the Southside. Also the youth on the Southside had a new pride and self-respect."

Evelyn replied, "Moses, your dream was very beautiful, but it was only a dream and not reality. I only wish it were a reality. I would love to see a revitalized black community here in River City."

Pastor Wright said, "Yes, I know my dream was only a dream but I'm going to try to make it a reality one day. This dream has inspired me to want to uplift the black community. I plan to lead a crusade to do it."

Evelyn replied, "Moses, I believe you can lead a crusade to uplift the black community. You are a very determined person once you make up your mind to do something."

Pastor Wright said, "Thanks, Baby, for the encouragement. In a few minutes I'm going to call Rev. Mays and tell him about my dream."

Pastor Wright immediately telephoned Rev. Mays and when he answered the telephone, Pastor Wright said to him, "Hello, Rev. Mays, this is Pastor Wright."

Rev. Mays replied, "Pastor Wright, my dear brother, is this really you calling me? How are you doing?"

Pastor Wright said, "I am doing fine, my brother. I called you to tell you about a beautiful dream I had last night."

Rev. Mays replied, "Tell me about this beautiful dream of yours, Pastor Wright. I'm very anxious to hear about it."

Pastor Wright said, "I dreamed last night that I saw a revitalized black community here on the Southside, and it was a beautiful sight. There were new black businesses and homes; there were rebuilt houses and apartments. The residents were believing in themselves and trying to achieve their goals. Also, I saw a new, positive attitude here on the Southside."

Rev. Mays replied, "My dear brother, that was a remarkable dream you had! I just wish it could become a reality."

Pastor Wright said, "Rev. Mays, I'm going to work as hard as I can to make my dream a reality. I am going to lead a crusade to uplift the black community. I hope to inspire as many people as possible to join this crusade. Of course, we will need money to uplift the black community. I believe we can get the money we need by establishing a Community Uplifting Fund. I hope we can get as many people as possible in the black community here on the

Southside to contribute to it. We will also need middle class blacks who have left the Southside for the suburb of Cypress Gardens to help us. If we can get the 'brothers and sisters' to come together for a common cause of uplifting the community, everything will work out fine."

Rev. Mays replied, "Pastor Wright, my dear brother, what you have just said is too good to be true. I can't believe it. I am so happy that I feel like shouting and praising God. Hallelujah!"

Pastor Wright said, "Yes, I plan to lead a crusade to uplift the black community and I believe with all my heart that it will be successful. I'm going to work, work, and work to make my dream a reality."

Rev. Mays replied, "Pastor Wright, my dear brother, I am touched by your sincere desire to want to uplift the black community. My congregation and I will return to Faith Missionary Baptist Church to work with you. We left you out of frustration but we are coming back to rejoin you. I believe a strong and united Faith Missionary Baptist Church can serve as a base of operation to uplift the black community. From this base of operation, we can work to bring the community together to reclaim our frustrated and abandoned youth, to rebuild our boarded-up apartments and homes, to open businesses, to help our struggling 'sisters' who are trying to raise kids without husbands, and to give hope to the hopeless."

Pastor Wright said, "I am so happy that you are returning to Faith Missionary Baptist Church. We missed you. The church hasn't been the same without you. Praise God! Praise God! With all of us at Faith Missionary Baptist Church working together, I believe we can inspire many others to join us for the common cause of uplifting the black community."

Rev. Mays replied, "Pastor Wright, my dear brother, we are going to return to Faith Missionary Baptist Church next Sunday. I will call the members who left with me and tell them the good news that we are going to reunite as one church."

Pastor Wright said, "Rev. Mays, calling the members who left with you and telling them the good news is the proper thing to do. Also spread the word to others that Faith Missionary Baptist Church is reuniting. In addition, spread the word that I have formally proclaimed next Sunday a day of forgiveness and reconciliation at our church. The Lord has blessed us to be able to get back together again. Very few churches are able to reunite once they split up."

Pastor Wright was now one happy man. He hadn't felt so good in a long time. He looked forward to his church being reunited next Sunday. He also looked forward to leading the crusade to uplift the black community.

When Sister Brown learned from Pastor Wright that Faith Missionary Baptist Church was reuniting, she became so happy that she burst into tears. She just sat in her chair at home and shed tears of joy.

The church split up last year had hurt Sister Brown more than anyone. No one loved Faith Missionary Baptist Church more than she did; no one loved Pastor Wright and Rev. Mays more than she did. Therefore, when the church split up last year and the two pastors quit talking to each other, she had been devastated. But now she was shedding tears of happiness for the soon-to-be church reunion.

After Sister Brown finished shedding her tears of happiness, she called her cousin Willie and told him she was coming over to his house to bring him and his wife Nora some good news. When Sister Brown arrived at the Spencer's residence, she was greeted warmly by them. The two were glad to see her. After hugging Willie and Nora, Sister Brown sat down on the sofa and said to them, "Guess what? I just heard from Pastor Wright that Faith Missionary Baptist

Church is reuniting. Rev. Mays and the members who left with him are returning next Sunday. Isn't that going to be something? Pastor Wright has proclaimed next Sunday as a day of forgiveness and reconciliation at our church."

Willie said, "Cousin Alice, it is so wonderful that we are getting back together. I believe Faith Missionary Baptist Church needs to get back together again."

Nora said, "Alice, I am so happy that our church is reuniting. Now, Willie and I can go to the same church again. It's a shame we had to split up in the first place. But sometimes things happen for a reason."

Sister Brown replied, "Willie and Nora, I have some more good news to tell you all. Pastor Wright had some kind of dream this past Friday night, and in it he saw a revitalized black community here in River City. This dream has inspired him to want to make it a reality. He plans to lead a crusade to uplift the black community. He is all fired-up over this dream. I have never seen him like this before."

Willie said, "Cousin Alice, you are kidding? Pastor Wright is going to lead a crusade to uplift the black community? That is hard to believe. You know, he and Rev. Mays fell out over his lack of leadership in the black community. But I'm very glad that his dream has inspired him to want to come down from the pulpit and go to work in the community. He is a dynamic man and I believe that if anyone can inspire black people to work together to improve their lives, he can. I look forward to working with him in his crusade to uplift the black community."

Nora said, "Alice, it is so beautiful that Pastor Wright is going to work to try to make his dream a reality. Many of our people are suffering, and I am going to do all I can to help make his dream come true."

When Sunday arrived, Faith Missionary Baptist Church was

packed. The huge crowd included members and non-members. They all wanted to be part of the great event, the day of forgiveness and reconciliation.

The day of forgiveness and reconciliation at Faith Missionary Baptist Church turned out to be the most memorable day in its history. The members who left and the members who remained were so happy to see each other again. They hugged each other; they shook hands with each other; and they sang and prayed. Some members got up and testified, thanking God for enabling them to forgive each other so they could come together again as one. Sister Brown was the happiest and most emotional member of them all. She shouted, she cried, and she got up and testified. Pastor Wright preached a very inspirational sermon. He thanked God for giving them the strength to forgive each other so they could reunite. He also said to the congregation, "Brothers and sisters, we have been truly tested by adversity these past fifteen months but we have triumphed over it. In fact, our split up was a blessing in disguise, because it has made us a stronger and more united church. We are an example of people in the black community who have learned how to forgive each other and reconcile our differences. I wish others in the black community would follow our example. If we, as a people, can forgive other peoples and show beautiful humanity to them, surely we can do this to each other."

After the day of forgiveness and reconciliation, Pastor Wright began working in earnest to make his dream of uplifting the black community a reality. He encouraged people to work hard to make their dreams a reality and not to be discouraged by adversity. He gave inspirational lectures at his church and elsewhere in the community, urging people to come together for the common cause of uplifting the Southside. He established the Community Uplifting Fund that he had been talking about and encouraged people to contribute to it. He also began having fund-raisers at his church to raise money for the Community Uplifting Fund.

Pastor Wright's crusade to uplift the black community had an immediate effect on the people of River City. People talked about him and his crusade all over town. They were inspired by his positive message of hope, self-reliance, and pride, and joined his crusade in large numbers.

Among the people who had heard his message and had come away inspired was none other than Harry, the hustler, himself. He had gone to Pastor Wright's church, heard his message, and had come away believing that he could turn his life around.

After visiting Pastor Wright's church, Harry, the hustler, decided to tell his good friends Walter, the wino, and Phyliss, the prostitute, about his inspirational experience. One evening while standing on the corner of 28th St. and Monroe Ave., he told them that he had been to Pastor Wright's church. He said to them, "Walter, Phyllis, guess what? I went to Pastor Wright's church last week and I enjoyed his speech about uplifting the black community. That man is really something."

Walter grinned and said, "Harry, man, did you really go to Pastor Wright's church? Come on, man, you are kidding me. I can't visualize Harry, the hustler, going to church. What is getting to be wrong with you? Are you trying to get saved?"

Phyllis, with a smirk on her face, asked, "Harry, did you knock on the church door?"

Harry said, "Walter, you and Phyllis are playing, but I am serious; I really enjoyed Pastor Wright's message. It's the kind of message I like to hear. His message inspired me and made me believe in myself again. If Pastor Wright can work to make his dream a reality, so can I. I've always dreamed of owning my own auto service shop, and I'm going to work to make my dream a reality. First, I'm going back to school and get my G.E.D. Then I'm going to take courses to become a mechanic. Afterward, I'm going to get myself a mechanic job, get some experience and save some money, then I'm going to open my own auto service shop. I believe I can do that. I'm not going to let anyone or anything turn me around. I am going to walk out on faith and make my dream a reality. I am no longer proud to be a hustler; I can do better than that. I'm tired of using being poor and hungry as a kid to justify my criminal activity; instead I'm going to take personal responsibility for it. I became a hustler because I wanted to become one. Now I'm going to turn my life around. Walter, Phyllis, this is my last day on this corner. Starting tomorrow I am no longer Harry the Hustler."

Walter said, "Harry, man, I've never heard you talk like this before. Your words have touched and inspired me. I haven't felt this positive in a long time. Harry, man, if you are going to try to turn your life around, so am I. I'm going to stop feeling sorry for myself and quit drinking this wine. I've been a miserable failure, standing on this corner and begging people for money to buy wine so it could help me cope with my shattered dream of being a pro basketball player. Yes, I've been wallowing in self-pity ever since I was kicked off the basketball team in college for using drugs, but I'm going to get up like a man and try to change my condition. Harry, man, if you are going to try to make your dream a reality, so am I. You know, my dream was to be a pro basketball player but I am too old to pursue that now. However, I am not too old to become a basketball coach and that is going to be my dream. I'm going to go back to college, complete my degree in physical education, and become a basketball coach. I believe I can do that. Also, I want to be a role model for the youth in this community. I want little boys to be able to look at me with pride and say, 'Look, there's Coach Walter Pierce. When I grow up I want to be just like him.' Harry, Phyllis, this is my last day on this corner too. Starting tomorrow I am no longer Walter the Wino."

Phyllis joined the conversation and said, "Harry, you and Walter are not going to leave me on this corner by myself. I know that for sure. If you can leave this corner, so can I. And furthermore, if you are going to try to turn your lives around, so am I. I'm going to stop feeling sorry for myself, too, and quit making excuses for becoming a prostitute. I became one because I wanted to. I also say that all men are no good, but I know that is not true. There are some good men out there; I just need to become a better selector of men. Harry, Walter, if you are going to work to make your dreams a reality, so am I. You know, I have always dreamed of becoming a schoolteacher, and I am going to work to make my dream a reality. I'm going back to school and get my G.E.D., then I'm going to college and get a degree in elementary education, and afterward I'm going to become an elementary schoolteacher. I believe I can do that. I want to become a beacon of hope for people who are wallowing in the muck and mire of criminal activity. I want a young hustler or a young prostitute to say, 'Look, there's Phyllis Carter she used to be a prostitute, but now she is a schoolteacher. If she can turn her life around, so can I.' Harry, Walter, this is our last time on the corner together. However, we need to stay in touch with each other."

Meanwhile, it was now April of 1998. Pastor Wright's crusade to uplift the black community had gone on for nine months and it was steadily gaining momentum. Thousands of people had joined the crusade and had pledged their commitment to it. Over $2 million had been raised for the Community Uplifting Fund. The crusade was also the talk of the town of River City and had brought thousands of people together for a common cause.

In early July, Pastor Wright announced that Faith Missionary Baptist Church would have a "wake up rally" to celebrate the first year of existence of the crusade to uplift the black community. The date was set for Saturday, July 25, 1998, at 7:00 p.m.

The "wake up rally" brought an overflow crowd to Faith Missionary Baptist Church. The huge crowd reflected a wide spectrum of people from the Southside and from the suburb of Cypress Gardens: teachers, ministers, doctors and lawyers, blue collar workers, laborers, hustlers, gang members, the unemployed, and the young and old. Some people who would normally have been out socializing and partying on a Saturday night were here. Some people who had been asleep and out of it for many years were here, they had been awaken by Pastor Wright's message. They all had come together for a common cause—to uplift the black community. The atmosphere in the church was like an old time revival meeting. There was speaking, singing, praying, and testifying. Sister Brown got up and thanked God for bringing all the people together so they could help themselves. Willie and Nora got up and talked about their commitment to the crusade to uplift the black community. Harry, Walter, and Phyllis got up and talked about how they had been inspired to turn their lives around, and pledged their support for Pastor Wright's crusade. Lots of people got up and made talks or gave testimonies. Finally it was time for Pastor Wright to give his lecture. He said to the crowd, "Brothers and sisters, thank you so much for coming out tonight to support the crusade to uplift the black community. It is going very well, much better than I expected at this point. We have raised over $4 millon for the Community Uplifting Fund. Thank you for your support. Although we have raised over 4 million dollars, we will need more to revitalize our community. We plan to use the money to rebuild all of the boarded-up houses and apartments in our community, to open new businesses that will create jobs for our unemployed, and to provide training and education for those who need it. We also need to reclaim our youth; many of them have gone astray out of frustration and hopelessness. We need to plan for the future of our children; they are our future as a people. The twenty-first century is less than two years away; we need to plan for it. The twenty-first century will become increasingly sophisticated, and those who are not prepared for it will be left behind. The Bible says, 'Where there is no vision the people perish.'"

Pastor Wright continued his inspirational lecture for two hours. It was interrupted numerous times by loud applause. The "wake up rally" ended with a prayer by Rev. Mays and the audience singing the song "Save the Children."

The Monday following the "wake up rally," Pastor Wright and others met at Faith Missionary Baptist Church to discuss the Community Uplifting Fund. Pastor Wright began the discussion by saying that it would take lots of sacrificing by many people to raise the funds needed to revitalize the black community. He then said he would set an example by ending his annual vacation to Jamaica, instead he would vacation here in the states. The money saved would be put into the Community Uplifting Fund. Rev. Mays said he would set an example by not buying a new Cadillac every year, instead he would buy one when he needed one. The money saved would be put into the Community Uplifting Fund. Sister Brown said she would set an example by not buying a new hat every week to wear to church on Sunday, instead she would buy one when she needed it. The money saved would be put into the Community Uplifting Fund. Willie said he would set an example by stop buying a lot of new clothes he didn't need and the money saved would be put into the Community Uplifting Fund. Nora said she was addicted to shopping and generally bought something each time she went shopping, even though she didn't need it. She said her aim in the future was to stop buying things she didn't need and the money saved would be put into the Community Uplifting Fund. One man said he would set an example by spending less on cigarettes and potato chips and the money saved would be put into the Community Uplifting Fund. One teenager said he would set an example by stop paying $200 for a pair of sneakers, instead he would pay much less for them and the money saved would be put into the Community Uplifting Fund. One man said that he lost at least $100 every week at the gambling casino trying to make the big hit. He said his aim in the future was to quit gambling and the money saved would be put into the Community Uplifting Fund. Others pledged to quit spending lots of money on liquor and drugs to help them cope with their problems, instead they would put this money into the Community Uplifting Fund so it could be used to help them solve their problems.

In late August, about a month after the "wake up rally," Willie and Nora were barbecuing in their backyard when Willie said to Nora, "Honey, that 'wake up rally' and the Community Uplifting Fund meeting were really something. I enjoyed them both. I believe Pastor Wright's dream to revitalize the black community is going to become a reality. In fact, he is working so hard that it has to become a reality."

Nora replied, "I believe his dream is going to become a reality too. Just think what it will mean for the Southside! For one thing a revitalized black community will bring us much pride. Even the children will be proud to have seen their parents, relatives, friends, and neighbors come together for a common cause of uplifting the community."

Willie said, "Nora, you are right. A revitalized black community, achieved by its own people, will definitely bring lots of pride to them. But if we hadn't moved back here in 1995, we would have missed being a part of this great crusade."

Nora replied, "Willie, I am so glad we moved back here to River City, Arkansas. I have enjoyed living here since we moved from Detroit and this crusade to uplift the community is so wonderful. It is just amazing how the people on the Southside and people from Cypress Gardens have come together for a common cause."

Willie said, "Nora, it sure is amazing how the people have all come together for a common cause of uplifting the community."

ANALYSIS OF STORY

The story "They All Came Together to Uplift the Community" revolves around people coming together for the common cause of uplifting the black community.

Willie and Nora left Detroit, Michigan after living there for thirty-four years and returned back home to River City, Arkansas to live. They found that the town had changed a lot. They also found that the black section of River City, the Southside, was plagued by drugs, crime and violence, and high rates of unemployment, problems it didn't have when they left thirty-four years ago.

After Willie and Nora joined Faith Missionary Baptist Church, it was hit by internal problems. Rev. Mays, the assistant pastor, was dissatisfied with the head pastor's lack of leadership in the black community. He wanted Pastor Wright, the pastor of Faith Missionary Baptist Church, to provide strong leadership in an effort to try to solve the black community's socioeconomic problems. However, Pastor Wright refused to accept the challenge of providing the necessary leadership to try to solve these problems. As a result, Rev. Mays and half of the members of Faith Baptist Church left Pastor Wright to start their own church.

In the meantime, Pastor Wright had a dream that inspired him to want to lead a crusade to revitalize a deteriorating black community. When Pastor Wright told Rev. Mays about his plan to lead a crusade to uplift the black community, he was overjoyed and decided to return with his members to reunite Faith Missionary Baptist Church. The church reunification was marked by a day of forgiveness and reconciliation. Pastor Wright, leading a strong and united church, was able to inspire many people to come together in a common effort to uplift the black community.

This story shows the importance of forgiveness and reconciliation, without it, it is very difficult to come together or stay together.

What is More Valuable than Silver and Gold?

▼▼

DURING THE 1890s AND EARLY 1900s, THOUSANDS OF BLACKS LEFT THE South and migrated West to Oklahoma. They were escaping the hard times and oppression of the South, and were hoping to find a safer and better life in Oklahoma, but it didn't always turn out that way.

This large influx of blacks into Oklahoma gave rise to black towns. Within a twenty year period, 1890 to 1910, around twenty-five black towns were established. They had names such as Boley, Langston City, and Clairview.

Another black town that was founded during this period was Happyville. It was founded in 1895. That year a group of blacks from Tennessee, who were friends and relatives, arrived in Oklahoma to begin a new life. After buying some land, they decided to call the settlement they were going to build Happyville.

The leaders of this close-knit group of blacks were two Civil War veterans, Frederick Allbright and L.T. Cotton. Frederick Allbright, fifty-two, was a carpenter and brickmason. L.T. Cotton, fifty-three, was a preacher. The two were also close friends, having fought together in a number of battles during the Civil War, including the Battle of Nashville and the battle at Milliken's Bend in Louisiana.

The newly arrived blacks struggled with racial prejudice and droughts their first few years in Oklahoma. But they were able to make it, thanks to strong leadership from their two leaders and thanks to the trust they had in each other, which made their system of sharing and caring possible.

By 1905 Happyville had grown from a small settlement to a thriving little farming town. It had a store, a cotton gin, a school, and other buildings. It was also surrounded by farmland that produced cotton, peanuts, sorghum, vegetables, poultry, and livestock in abundance.

In 1913 Happyville lost one of its founding leaders, Mr. Frederick Allbright, who died at the age of seventy. He was, more than anyone else, responsible for the survival of Happyville in its difficult early years. He had inspired everyone with his great spirit of determination. His death caused much sadness in the town.

Meanwhile, Happyville continued to grow and attract people to it. In 1920 a Tulsa newspaper described Happyville as a thriving Negro town of around 2,000 inhabitants, with a bank, a newspaper, four churches, a cotton gin, two hotels, two schools, and numerous other buildings. It also had a number of professional people, including several doctors and lawyers.

Although Happyville was a symbol of prosperity in 1920 with its successful businesses, its most valuable asset was the trust among its inhabitants. Trust was what made Happyville's system of sharing and caring so successful. Everyone in the community trusted each other. Storeowners didn't hesitate to sell farmers things on credit because they knew they would be repaid. People didn't hesitate to loan their neighbors sugar, flour, molasses or money because they knew they would be repaid. People didn't hesitate to leave their doors unlocked when they left home because they knew their neighbors would keep a watchful eye out for them. In short, the spirit of trust among its inhabitants was what made Happyville tick.

In April of 1925, Happyville was saddened by the sudden death of Rev. L.T. Cotton, its other founding leader. He had been very instrumental to the survival of Happyville in its difficult beginning with his inspirational sermons of hope and faith.

In October of 1929 the nation was hit by the Great Depression. Happyville was immediately effected by the Great Depression and went into a state of decline. Within two years most of its businesses closed and nearly half of its inhabitants moved away. Throughout the 1930s the town of Happyville continued to decline. Many town people suffered from unemployment and many nearby farmers had to deal with soil erosion and attacks on their cotton crops by insects called boll weevils. But despite all of the adversity, the people of Happyville never gave up and survived the gloomy 1930s. By 1945, the year World War II ended, Happyville had fully recovered from its state of decline and was once again a thriving farming community.

In May of 1946, on a Saturday morning, a tall, dark, handsome stranger rode into Happyville driving a brand-new pink Cadillac. He was sharper than sharp—wearing a flashy, black, pin-striped suit; a stylish, black hat with a white feather in it; a pair of spit-polished black shoes; a sparkling diamond ring; and a fancy gold watch. He was also charming and very friendly, speaking or nodding to everyone he met in town. He said his name was Marvin McKinley, he had just stopped in Happyville for a few days, and he was on his way home to Oklahoma City.

Marvin McKinley, tall, dark, handsome, and sharply dressed,

created quite a sensation among the women in Happyville that Saturday. They could be heard whispering to each other about how handsome and charming he was. Some of the young, single women could be seen openly flirting with him.

All the attention he received from the women in Happyville stroked Marvin's ego and one could tell that he was enjoying it. However, the woman who caught his attention was Mrs. Carmen Stokes, the prettiest and wealthiest woman in town. Upon seeing her coming out of the bank, he immediately introduced himself to her. He told her how pretty and fine she was, how much he liked her, and how much he would like to get to know her. She admired his self-confidence and was flattered by his nice compliments of her, and told him she would also like to get to know him. By mutual consent, the two agreed to get acquainted the next day over a meal at Rose's Restaurant down the street.

Mrs. Carmen Stokes was the granddaughter of Frederick Allbright, one of the founding leaders of Happyville, and the daughter of Roscoe Allbright, his son. The Allbrights were the wealthiest family in town, owning lots of land and the only bank in town, Freedom's Bank.

Meanwhile, that Sunday evening, while eating a delicious meal, Marvin and Carmen got acquainted. Carmen told Marvin that she was twenty-seven years old, a college graduate with a degree in accounting, and was manager of Freedom's Bank in town. She also told him that she was a recent divorcee, having divorced her husband the previous year. Marvin told Carmen that he was twenty-nine years old, single, and a college graduate with a degree in clothing and textiles. He also told her that he had gotten out of the U.S. Army in March of 1944, and for the past two years he had been working and taking business courses in Baltimore, Maryland; now he was on his way home to Oklahoma City to look for a job.

After Marvin told Carmen that he was looking for a job, she thought for a while, then she said, "Marvin, we have an accountant position opening here at Freedom's Bank. Although you have a degree in clothing and textiles, you still qualify because you have a college degree and courses in business. We will train you to become an accountant."

Marvin, smiling broadly, said, "Carmen, I will gladly accept the position. I look forward to working at Freedom's Bank with you."

Marvin and Carmen became better acquainted with each other while working together at Freedom's Bank. They learned more about each other's past. They began to go to lunch together everyday at Rose's Restaurant. Soon they could be seen holding hands while walking around town. As the weeks passed, the two grew closer together. When fall arrived, they began going out of town to college football games together. By Christmas tall, dark, handsome Marvin McKinley had captured Carmen's heart, and she was crazy in love with him.

In all fairness to Carmen, she was not the only person in Happyville under the spell of Marvin McKinley's charm, many others were also. The teenage boys and girls admired his smooth and hip talk, and said he was "one cool dude". Many old women in town admired his friendliness and kindness, and said he was a nice young man. The young women in town admired his good looks and magnetic personality, and said they wished they could be Mrs. Carmen Stokes. Many men in town admired his flashy style and self-confidence, and tried to imitate him. The mayor and entire town council admired his poise and good speaking ability, and said he would make a good politician.

By the spring of 1947, Marvin McKinley had almost the whole town of Happyville under the influence of his charm except for a few people, who still had some doubts about him. One person who was somewhat skeptical of him was Rev. Joseph Cotton. He was the grandson of Rev. L.T. Cotton, one of the founding leaders of the town. Rev. Joseph Cotton told the townspeople that he thought they were going too fast with a person they didn't know very well and they should be a little more cautious with him. Another person who was skeptical of Marvin McKinley was none other than Earnest "Big Junior" Coleman, thirty, single, businessman and owner of Happyville's largest store. Big Junior was openly critical and suspicious of Marvin McKinley. He told the townspeople, who would listen, that Marvin McKinley wasn't the nice person he pretended to be. Big Junior said to them, "You all better listen to me. I'm warning you now. That 'Pretty Boy' Marvin McKinley is up to something. He isn't hanging around this small country town of ours for nothing. He's too nice. He's hiding something behind that niceness. I've said it once and I'm going to say it again. That rascal is up to something."

Despite Big Junior's warnings to the people of Happyville that "Pretty Boy" Marvin McKinley was up to something, very few of them took his warnings seriously. The reason was they believed his jealousy of "Pretty Boy" Marvin's romance with Carmen Stokes had clouded his judgement and was causing him to say negative things about him. The people of Happyville were aware that Big Junior had tried to court Carmen but she had rejected him in a nice way, whereas she had been strongly attracted to "Pretty Boy" Marvin the moment she first saw him. Therefore, because "Pretty Boy" Marvin had beat Big Junior's time with Carmen, most of the people of Happyville thought that was why Big Junior constantly cried "that rascal is up to something." In short, most of the people of Happyville thought Big Junior's jealousy of "Pretty Boy" Marvin's successful romance with Carmen Stokes was the reason he was so suspicious of his intentions.

To be truthful about the situation, Big Junior was jealous of "Pretty Boy" Marvin's successful romance with Carmen Stokes. Big Junior had repeatedly tried to date Carmen after she divorced her husband, but she had always rejected him in a nice way. She would say, "Big Junior, I'm still trying to get over my break up with my husband. When I'm ready to date again, I will let you know." But what had enraged Big Junior so much was the moment "Pretty Boy" Marvin came to town, she had immediately begun to date him, whereas she had slyly rejected him. This situation led Big Junior to believe that she thought he wasn't good enough. But instead of getting angry with Carmen for slyly rejecting him, Big Junior had gotten angry with "Pretty Boy" Marvin for romancing a woman who didn't want him. However, the reason Big Junior hadn't become angry with Carmen was because he was secretly in love with her, which had made him blind to her faults. Therefore, he had displaced his anger for Carmen to "Pretty Boy" Marvin.

Big Junior's love for Carmen made him jealous of "Pretty Boy" Marvin. The sight of "Pretty Boy" Marvin and Carmen walking around town together holding hands aroused jealousy in him. The sight of "Pretty Boy" Marvin driving Carmen's car around town aroused much jealousy in him. The rumor that Carmen bought "Pretty Boy" Marvin clothes and gave him money aroused much jealousy in him. But the rumor that "Pretty Boy" Marvin had Carmen wrapped around his finger and used her like a tool made him very jealous and angry.

Although Big Junior was very jealous of "Pretty Boy" Marvin's successful romance with Carmen, he could still see he wasn't the nice person he pretended to be. He could see that "Pretty Boy" Marvin was using Carmen and didn't care as much for her as she thought. When Carmen came into his store to buy something, Big Junior would sometimes take her aside and say to her, "Carmen, that dude you are courting is just using you. He doesn't care as much for you as you think."

Carmen would reply, "Big Junior, stay out of my business."

Meanwhile, tension was beginning to build between Big Junior and "Pretty Boy" Marvin over Carmen. Whenever Big Junior saw "Pretty Boy" Marvin in town, he would give him a mean look. Whenever "Pretty Boy" Marvin and Carmen walked around town together and met Big Junior, "Pretty Boy" Marvin would intentionally put his arm around Carmen's shoulder and wink at Big Junior. Sometimes "Pretty Boy" Marvin would try to play the nice guy role when he met Big Junior on the street, and would say to him, "Hello, Big Junior, how are you doing today?" Big Junior would give him a mean look and walk on.

As the weeks passed, the tension between the two continued to build. Big Junior would give "Pretty Boy" Marvin icy looks when they met on the street. "Pretty Boy" Marvin would sometimes come into Big Junior's store with Carmen at his side and would taunt Big Junior by kissing Carmen softly on the lips or by holding her hand. These subtle taunts would make Big Junior's blood boil with anger. By summer the tension between the two rivals had reached a peak.

On a Saturday morning in late June "Pretty Boy" Marvin and Carmen walked into Big Junior's store. They browsed around for awhile in the store, then "Pretty Boy" Marvin said, "Carmen, that sure is a pretty hat there."

Carmen replied, "Marvin, it sure is. Do you want it?"

"Pretty Boy" Marvin said, "Yes, Honey, I sure do."

Carmen picked up the stylish hat, went to the cash register, and paid for it. This made Big Junior very angry, and before he could catch himself, he said, "Carmen, can't you see that this man is using you? All he wants is what you can give him."

There was silence, then "Pretty Boy" Marvin said to Big Junior, "Well, well, well, guess who is sticking his nose into our business, Mr. Country Bumpkin himself. Say, Mr. Country Bumpkin, you are sticking your nose into our business where it doesn't belong, and I don't like that. It is none of your business when my honey buys me a pretty hat."

Big Junior said, "It may not be my business, but I am making it my business. I am tired of you using my homegirl. You had better quit using her if you know what is good for you."

"Pretty Boy" Marvin laughed sarcastically and replied, "Say what? Country Bumpkin, who are you to tell me what to do? Just look at you, wearing that used car salesman suit and sporting that cheap farmer's haircut. You can't tell me what to do. You have never been anywhere. I doubt if you have ever been outside the state of Oklahoma. Look at me, I've been all over the world. I've fought in battles in Europe, North Africa, and Asia. I'm an international man."

Big Junior said, "You may be an international man, but you don't have anything. You are a rolling stone, and gaining nothing. Look at me, I own a store, I am my own boss. Carmen is your boss at Freedom's Bank. And furthermore, she is always buying you things. In other words she is your means of support. You are a man who is depending upon a woman for support."

Big Junior's biting criticism angered "Pretty Boy" Marvin and hurt his pride. He didn't like being told that even though it was true. He looked angrily at Big Junior and said, "Well, well, well, look who is trying to put me down, Mr. Country Bumpkin himself, wearing cheap high-water pants and a coat with sleeves halfway up his arms. Man, buy yourself a suit that will fit you. Big Junior, you are about as country as they come. Just look at you with that mud on your shoes. Ha ha ha ha!"

"Pretty Boy" Marvin's nasty remarks set Big Junior's blood to boiling and he said angrily, "I may be country, I may not wear fancy clothes, I may not drive a flashy car; but I tell you what, 'Pretty Boy,' you can't whip my country behind. Let's step outside this store and see who is the better man. I believe that I am the better man. I will wallow you all over the ground. I've been itching to whip your pretty behind. If you step outside this store, you won't be a pretty boy anymore."

"Pretty Boy" Marvin laughed sarcastically and taunted, "Well, well, well, just look who is trying to rhyme and talk stuff, Mr. Country Bumpkin himself, saying he wants to whip my behind. Well, I tell you what, Big Junior, if you want to fight, we can get it on. I have never been a person to back down from a fight. In fact, I've been wanting to whip your country behind for months. Big Junior, listen, and listen well, you are not challenging an ordinary dude, you are challenging Marvin McKinley."

Big Junior laughed sarcastically and replied, "'Pretty Boy,' you have it backward; you don't know whom you are messing with. You are messing with Earnest 'Big Junior' Coleman and they don't call me 'Big Junior' for nothing."

"Pretty Boy" Marvin said, "Big Junior, you are one big dude, but your size doesn't scare me. You know they say the bigger you are, the harder you fall."

Big Junior bursting with anger, replied, " You talk some mighty tough talk 'Pretty Boy,' but you can't be that bad. Let's step outside and see how bad you are. I want to see if you can back up your tough talk. And furthermore, I'm tired of talking; I'm ready for some action. Leave your switchblade in your pocket and come outside and fight me like a man."

"Pretty Boy" Marvin said, "Country Bumpkin, I don't need a weapon to whip you. It will be a pleasure to whip your country behind."

Big Junior and "Pretty Boy" Marvin walked outside the store, then began arguing again. Their loud arguing drew a crowd. Both men were seething with anger. Suddenly, Big Junior hit "Pretty Boy" Marvin with a hard right that knocked him to the ground. The blow surprised "Pretty Boy" Marvin, but he got up and hit Big Junior with a thundering right that knocked him to the ground. "Pretty Boy" Marvin then dove on Big Junior and the two combatants began wrestling furiously on the ground. While wrestling on the ground, Big Junior, using his weight, maneuvered himself on top of "Pretty Boy" Marvin and began punching him in the face, but "Pretty Boy" Marvin was too good a fighter to be held down, he subsequently knocked Big Junior off of him with a hard right. The two combatants then got up off the ground and began boxing, landing jabs and heavy rights to each other. After their furious exchange of blows the two combatants began wrestling again and fell to the ground. The evenly matched, heavyweight championship like fight went on and on, Big Junior would have the advantage, then "Pretty Boy" Marvin would have the advantage, but neither one could deliver the knock out blow to the other to end the fight. With the crowd around them hooping and hollering and urging them on, Big Junior and "Pretty Boy" Marvin fought furiously until they were both bruised and exhausted. Then they just lay on the ground too tired to move.

News of the furious fight between Big Junior and "Pretty Boy" Marvin spread quickly through the town of Happyville. People who had seen it described it as one hell of a fight, the likes of which Happyville had never witnessed before. They also described it as ending in a draw, with neither man being able to deliver the knock-out blow to the other. However, Big Junior was blamed for starting the fight. People said that he had started an argument with "Pretty

Boy" Marvin over Carmen, then he had challenged him to a fight, and had struck the first blow.

The fight had an impact on the credibility of Big Junior and "Pretty Boy" Marvin in town. It hurt Big Junior's credibility, whereas it helped "Pretty Boy" Marvin's credibility. Since Big Junior was seen as having started the fight with "Pretty Boy" Marvin, no one in town believed him when he cried, "I'm warning you now! That 'Pretty Boy' Marvin is up to something." The people dismissed his warnings because they believed he was saying them out of jealousy of "Pretty Boy" Marvin. But on the other hand, the fight enhanced "Pretty Boy" Marvin's credibility in town. The few people in town who had earlier been somewhat skeptical of him because of Big Junior's warnings were now talking in his favor. They said that he was a nice guy and Big Junior talked negative about him because he was jealous of his successful relationship with Carmen Stokes. Even Rev. Joseph Cotton, the pastor of Happyville's A.M.E. Church, the largest and most influential church in town, was now singing his praises. In the barbershop, he was overheard saying some good things about him. He said, "I was mistaken earlier about the young man named Marvin McKinley. I was skeptical of him, but now I believe he has good intentions. He is an outstanding young man. Big Junior says these negative things about him because he is jealous of his successful relationship with the young lady, Carmen Stokes."

Soon after his favorable words about "Pretty Boy" Marvin, Rev. Joseph Cotton began to develop a friendship with him. They fished together and swapped war stories. Rev. Joseph Cotton told "Pretty Boy" Marvin about his soldier days in World War I and "Pretty Boy" Marvin told him about his soldier days in World War II.

The fight also drew "Pretty Boy" Marvin and Carmen closer together. They became inseparable. In mid-August "Pretty Boy" Marvin and Carmen went on a three-week vacation to California.

When they returned home in September, they told the people of Happyville how much they had enjoyed themselves. They also talked about getting married.

One Friday evening, about a week after their return from vacationing, "Pretty Boy" Marvin and Carmen were eating dinner at Rose's Restaurant when he said, "Carmen, I've been thinking about our relationship; I think it is so beautiful. You know I love you very much and would give you the world if I could. In fact, if I had only one wish that could come true, it would be to spend my life with you. Carmen, how much do you love me?"

Carmen replied, "Marvin, you don't have to ask me that question. You know how much I love you."

"Pretty Boy" Marvin said, "Come on, Carmen, tell me how much you love me."

Carmen replied, "Marvin, I love you more than anything else in the world and you know that. I've told you that many times before."

"Pretty Boy" Marvin said, "Carmen, I know you have told me that many times before, but I just like to hear you say it."

"Pretty Boy" Marvin paused and took a bite of the tasty steak on his plate, then he said, "Carmen, you know, I have been thinking about the future of the town of Happyville. It is a small farming town without any industry. I believe it needs some industry to grow. I have an idea. I would like to try to establish a factory here that makes clothes. I have a college degree in clothing and textiles, and I know how to make clothes. Carmen, you have seen some of the pretty suits I have made on your sewing machine. You know I am good."

Carmen replied, " Yes, Marvin, I know you are good at making clothes. I've seen them."

"Pretty Boy" Marvin said, "Carmen, I'm going to need your help in establishing this factory here in Happyville. Together as a team, we can do it."

Carmen asked, "Marvin, how can I help you?"

"Pretty Boy" Marvin answered, "I would like for you to help me borrow a loan from Freedom's Bank. You are the manager of the bank, you have pull, and you can help me get that loan. It is going to take money to build a clothing factory and get equipment for it. Carmen, I'm sure you can talk your father, who's the president of the bank, into loaning me some money. It is for a good cause. A factory will create jobs here in Happyville. I need to borrow at least $15,000 to get started."

Carmen said, "Marvin, $15,000 is a lot of money. I'm not sure I can talk my father into loaning you that much money. But I will try."

Carmen talked to her father about "Pretty Boy" Marvin's plan to establish a factory in Happyville and his desire to borrow $15,000. But she was unable to convince him to loan "Pretty Boy" Marvin the money. He said to her, "Carmen, I know Marvin is a nice guy, but I need to talk to him before I decide to loan him that much."

The next evening Carmen's father, Mr. Allbright, sat down with "Pretty Boy" Marvin to discuss loaning him some money. "Pretty Boy" Marvin began the conversation by saying, "Mr. Allbright, I would like to borrow $15,000 from Freedom's Bank to help finance building a clothing factory here. This factory will be an asset to the community of Happyville. It will create jobs and attract other industry here. When the youth of Happyville finish school, they have very few opportunities to work here because of a lack of jobs. Some remain here but work in other towns, whereas others relocate in other towns and cities to work. This is called the brain drain. Some of Happyville's brightest young people help other towns and cities to grow and develop. But if we begin to industrialize Happyville, that will keep most of our brightest kids home, and they will use their education and skills to help Happyville grow and develop. Mr. Allbright, a $15,000 loan to me is an investment in the future of Happyville."

Mr. Allbright said, "Marvin, your idea about creating an industry here in Happyville sounds great. I believe we need to start doing something about our brightest minds leaving here to seek job opportunities in other towns and cities because of a lack of job opportunities here in Happyville. Marvin, you have convinced me to loan you $15,000."

"Pretty Boy" Marvin said, "Thank you so much Mr. Allbright for your approval of a $15,000 loan to help finance the establishing of a clothing factory here in Happyville. Again, thank you so much Mr. Allbright!"

Inspired by the approval of the $15,000 loan with Freedom's Bank, "Pretty Boy" Marvin began to tell others in town about his idea to establish a clothing factory in Happyville and encouraged them to invest in the project. Some people in town told him they liked the idea and would invest in the project, whereas others were a little skeptical of the project.

When "Big Junior" Coleman heard that "Pretty Boy" Marvin wanted to establish a clothing factory in Happyville and was encouraging people to invest money in the project, he was skeptical. He said building a clothing factory in Happyville was a good idea but he was skeptical of the person leading the drive to build the clothing factory. He also said he didn't trust "Pretty Boy" Marvin with all the money Freedom's Bank was going to loan him, and Mr. Allbright shouldn't have approved the loan of $15,000 to that rascal. Big Junior said to the people of Happyville, "You all better listen to me. I'm warning you now! That 'Pretty Boy' Marvin is up to something. I don't trust him at all. You all are crazy if you trust him with all that money. He's hiding something behind that niceness.

I've said it once and I'm going to say it again. That rascal is up to something!"

The people of Happyville might have listened to Big Junior a year ago, but his credibility had been damaged by his recent fight with "Pretty Boy" Marvin in which he was seen as the aggressor and they, therefore, ignored his warnings. They said he was saying those negative things about "Pretty Boy" Marvin because he was jealous of his success in courting Carmen Stokes.

In mid-October the leaders of Happyville invited the whole town to come to a town hall meeting in the school auditorium to discuss investing money in "Pretty Boy" Marvin's clothing factory project. They invited "Pretty Boy" Marvin to speak and explain his project to establish a clothing factory in Happyville, after which their would be a discussion.

It was a warm Friday evening when "Pretty Boy" Marvin and Carmen walked into the school auditorium for the town hall meeting. Marvin wore a stylish blue suit and Carmen wore a pretty blue dress. When "Pretty Boy" Marvin stepped up to the podium to speak, the auditorium got very quiet. "Pretty Boy" Marvin said to the crowd, "Thank you, brothers and sisters for coming out this evening. We have come out for a good cause. Our town of Happyville is a small farming town, but in order to grow, it needs industry. My aim is to establish a clothing factory here, which will create jobs for the people of Happysville. I believe if we establish an industry here, it will attract other industries. However, establishing an industry here in Happyville will cost money. I encourage you to invest in this clothing factory. I'm not going to try to tell you how much money to invest, but I will tell you this: invest as much money as you can, and then try to invest just a little bit more. The more money you invest in this clothing factory, the better off it will be. If we invest in this clothing factory, we will be investing in the future of Happyville and the future of its youth."

"Pretty Boy" Marvin was very inspiring and persuasive in his speech and after he finished speaking, lots of people in Happyville pledged to invest money in establishing the clothing factory. The investors included the town's mayor; the entire town council; Rev. Joseph Cotton, the town's most influential minister; and many others.

The next day after the town hall meeting, "Pretty Boy" Marvin announced that he was going to Oklahoma City on a business trip. There he planned to contact a company about building the clothing factory and equipping it. He told the people of Happyville that he would return in a week and tell them how everything had gone.

In late October "Pretty Boy" Marvin returned from Oklahoma City. In an informal town meeting he discussed his business trip. He said to the people, "Brothers and sisters, I have contacted Hudson Construction Enterprises in Oklahoma City, and they are going to build and equip the factory. However, you all know cash money talks. If we can come up with cash money, Hudson Construction Enterprises will begin immediately constructing our factory, and it will be finished by spring. The quicker we build the factory, the quicker we can begin making clothes. Also, Hudson Construction Enterprises will market the clothes we make in our factory all over Oklahoma and Texas. So, what I'm saying brothers and sisters, the quicker we gather the cash money the better off we will be."

The people of Happyville had absolute trust in "Pretty Boy" Marvin and agreed to provide him with the cash money so the project could get started immediately. Freedom's Bank gave him the $15,000 loan in cash money and the people of Happyville collectively gave him $10,000 cash in investment money.

In early November "Pretty Boy" Marvin told the people of Happyville that he was going to Oklahoma City to finalize the business deal with Hudson Construction Enterprises. He told everyone good-bye, hugged and kissed Carmen, and said he would return from Oklahoma City within a week. He then got into his pink Cadillac, put the briefcase carrying the $25,000 at his side, smiled and waved to everyone, and drove off, heading to Oklahoma City.

After a week had passed, "Pretty Boy" Marvin hadn't returned from Oklahoma City but the people of Happyville weren't worried, they believed that finalizing the business deal had taken him longer than he had expected, and he would return soon. When another week had passed and he still hadn't returned, some of the people in town began to worry. They said, "Marvin McKinley still hasn't returned from Oklahoma City; we hope nothing bad has happened to him. He was carrying a lot of cash money. Maybe, we should have written a check instead of letting him carry so much cash money." When three weeks had passed and he still hadn't returned from Oklahoma City, many people in town began to say that they believed something real bad had happened to him, and he wasn't going to return. Worried, they contacted law enforcement officials and put a missing person's report out on him, but the search came up empty. No one had seen or talked to a person named Marvin McKinley who matched the description they had given to law enforcement officials. It seemed like he had disappeared into thin air.

The sad news worried Carmen very much and she doubted if she would ever see her precious love again. She frantically searched his apartment for any kind of information he might have left behind that would explain where he had gone or would give more information about him. She searched through his clothes and letters he had left behind but could find nothing that could help her. Suddenly, something told her to search the closet again, this time more carefully. When she searched the closet again she found a suit coat of his that she had overlooked at first. She examined the pockets of the coat and found in his inside coat pocket a letter that he had forgotten to mail. She began reading the letter and it said, "Dear Luther, I am now living in a little, Negro country town called Happyville here in Oklahoma. Man, you won't believe how innocent and trusting the people are in this town. They believe everything I tell them. I am courting a pretty woman and she is wealthy, too. Her name is Carmen Stokes. She believes everything I tell her. She also buys me whatever I want. When the time comes, it will be easy to trick the country bumpkins in this town out of their money. Goodbye. I'll see you soon in Oklahoma City."

The cruel letter "Pretty Boy" Marvin left behind devastated Carmen and the town of Happyville. They couldn't believe that he was a phony. He had been so warm and friendly and had convinced them that he was a nice guy that could be trusted. They had believed him when he said he wanted to establish a clothing factory in Happyville that would create jobs. They had trusted him when he said he was going to use their $25,000 to help pay for building and equipping the factory. But he had let them down and betrayed their trust.

Because of their negative experience with "Pretty Boy" Marvin, many people in Happyville began to be distrustful and suspicious of each other. They became afraid to loan each other money and to share things.

When Rev. Joseph Cotton spoke at a town meeting, he talked about the damage "Pretty Boy" Marvin had done to the town of Happyville. He said, "We thought Marvin McKinley was a nice guy and a man of integrity, but he fooled us and turned out to be the crook Big Junior said he was. Big Junior was the only person in town who could see through his clever game of deception. Marvin McKinley completely fooled us, but we will never be fooled like that again. We will learn from our mistake. Marvin McKinley, with his greed and deceitfulness, has destroyed the most valuable asset we had in Happyville, which was trust. Our town was founded on trust. It was the main reason our town was able to survive its difficult early years. Because we trusted each other, we knew we could always depend upon each other during times of trouble and adversity. Trust has been more valuable to us than silver and gold. Now that trust has been destroyed."

Because of the spirit of distrust in town, the winter of 1947-48 was rough on the people of Happyville. Many people suffered because they couldn't get credit. Storeowners that traditionally let everyone have food, clothing, tools, and other items on credit were very selective to the people they gave credit to. Some residents refused to let their neighbors borrow things from them because they were afraid they wouldn't get them back in return. This selfishness caused some residents to show resentment toward their neighbors for not sharing with them and they, therefore, quit speaking to them.

When spring arrived the negative spirit of distrust was still effecting the town of Happyville, which made twelve year old "Little Johnny" Allbright very sad. He was very sad because he remembered when the town was filled with a spirit of happiness and trust. Just last spring the people were speaking and waving to each other, laughing and talking with each other, and sharing and caring with each other. Now many of them were sullen and selfish.

The thoughts of happier times in Happyville made "Little Johnny" want to bring them back. He, therefore, began to work to restore trust in Happyville. He encouraged his classmates at school to trust and share with each other. He got up in Happyville's A.M.E. Church, to the surprise of everyone, and gave inspirational talks, encouraging his fellow church members to love and trust each other. He greeted people on the street and in stores, urging them to work to bring trust back to Happyville. As the weeks passed, "Little Johnny's" efforts began to have an effect on the town. Many people once again began to laugh and talk with each other, and to speak to each other, but things still weren't back to normal.

One day while "Little Johnny" was at school, an idea came to him on how to further bring the town together. His idea was to have a picnic and invite everyone in the community to participate so they could kiss and make up, and come together again. "Little Johnny" told his classmates about his idea and they thought it was a good one to bring the town together again. Soon he and his classmates circulated the news about the picnic to everyone in town.

The town picnic took place in mid-June. It seemed like all the residents of Happyville and surrounding farms were there. The children had a wonderful time running and playing with each other. The adults were glad to see each other. Soon they were laughing and talking like old times. There was plenty of delicious food to share with each other and everyone enjoyed eating it. The people of Happyville had such a great time at the picnic that it was night before everyone went home. The picnic had done its job. It had brought the town together again.

By early August things were back to normal in Happyville. The people were speaking and waving to each other, laughing and talking with each other, and sharing and caring with each other. These were signs that trust had been completely restored in Happyville.

The restoration of trust in Happyville made Rev. Joseph Cotton very happy. At church, he told his congregation how happy he was to see trust restored in town. He said to them, "Brothers and sisters, I am so happy to see trust restored in our community. Isn't it a blessing that we have come together again? I am so proud of our town for having the strength to overcome the adversity that hit us last year. Even though we lost $25,000, we have something that is more valuable than silver and gold and it is called trust. Our town was founded on trust and that is what, more than anything else, has helped it to survive. We thank 'Little Johnny' Allbright for helping to restore trust in Happyville. Without his great effort, we still might be mired in a condition of distrust and suspicion. It is amazing how he has been able to bring us together. Let's give him a warm round of applause."

The church gave "Little Johnny" Allbright a standing ovation for his great effort in helping to restore trust in Happyville. After the standing ovation, he got up and bowed to the congregation and said, "Thank you all for your warm appreciation of my efforts; I love you so very much."

Meanwhile, ten months have passed since "Pretty Boy" Marvin manipulated the town of Happyville out of $25,000; yet law enforcement officials have been unable to find him. One day in early September a law enforcement official contacted Rev. Joseph Cotton about Marvin McKinley. He said to him, "Rev. Cotton, we have been searching for Marvin McKinley for months and have been unable to find him. We assure you, however, that he will be eventually caught."

The next day Rev. Cotton told Big Junior that the law was still searching for Marvin McKinley. Big Junior said, "That 'Pretty Boy' Marvin is sure hard to find with his slick self. It is unforgivable what he did to the people of Happyville. I tell you what Rev. Cotton, I'm going to Oklahoma City next week to search for him."

Rev. Cotton said, "Big Junior, I understand your frustration and impatience, but the law will eventually find him. Let the law find him."

Big Junior said, "Rev. Cotton, you are right. I should let the law find him but I want to see him behind bars so bad that I'm going to Oklahoma City to search for him. If I don't find him, I just don't find him. I have nothing to lose."

The next week Big Junior got in his car and drove to Oklahoma City. There, he went into the black section of town and searched for a week, asking people had they seen a tall, dark, handsome man named Marvin McKinley who drove a pink Cadillac and wore flashy clothes. But no one knew a Marvin McKinley that matched that description. Disappointed, Big Junior got in his car and headed for home.

When Big Junior got back to Happyville, he told Rev. Cotton that his search to find "Pretty Boy" Marvin had come up empty. Rev. Cotton said, "Big Junior, I figured your search would come up empty but you get an 'A' for your effort. Marvin McKinley might be anywhere now. Trying to find him is like looking for a needle in a haystack. If I were you, I would let the law find him. Looking for him could be dangerous. I am sure he is armed."

Big Junior replied, "Rev. Cotton, I should let the law find him but I'm a stubborn fellow and I'm going to try to find him again. However, on the next search for him, I'm going to use a different strategy."

Rev. Cotton said, "Big Junior, I hope you find him on your next search. Be careful and good luck."

After his conversation with Rev. Cotton, Big Junior went home and began to think about his strategy for finding "Pretty Boy" Marvin. He thought to himself, "I am aware that 'Pretty Boy' Marvin is a clever cookie. The name Marvin McKinley is probably a false name he is using and is not his real name. He might even be using several false names. This time I'm going to use a different strategy to search for him when I return to Oklahoma City. My strategy is to go into different places and listen with an alert ear to hear what I can pick up about him. I might find out something by chance. The old strategy of going around asking people do they know

Marvin McKinley failed because that is probably not his real name."

In early October Big Junior returned to the black section of Oklahoma City. He went into many different places, including restaurants, nightclubs, taverns, pool halls, and barbershops with his ears pricked up, hoping someone would say something that would lead him to "Pretty Boy" Marvin. However, in a whole week of listening in many different places, he couldn't pick up anything that would lead him to "Pretty Boy" Marvin. Frustrated, Big Junior decided to leave immediately for home. But his stomach started to growl and he changed his mind and went into a place called Henry's Café to eat lunch. While sitting there eating his food, Big Junior noticed two sharply-dressed men sitting at a table on the right side of him, they were eating and talking. The tall man said to the short man, "Say man, when was the last time you saw Christopher Stephens?"

The short man replied, "Man, I saw him about three months ago down in New Orleans. He is the same slick Christopher Stephens that you know. However, he is not driving his pink Cadillac anymore, instead he is driving a brand-new, black 1948 Ford car. It is pretty too."

The words "pink Cadillac" caught Big Junior's attention and he began to listen more intensely to the two men's conversation, while at the same time pretending not to be listening to them.

The short man continued to talk about Christopher Stephens, he said, "You know, Christopher Stephens changes cars like he changes women. He always has a pretty car and he always has a pretty woman. From the way he was dressed and the way he was flashing money when I saw him in New Orleans, it seemed like he had conned someone out of lots of money. He told me to meet him next week in Dallas at a big, fancy nightclub called the Supreme.

We are supposed to party and have a lot of fun there together."

The tall man smiled and replied, "So, Christopher Stephens is doing all right for himself. That is good. I sure would like to see my homeboy, that slick rascal."

The short man laughed at the mention of the words "slick rascal". He then said to the tall man, "Come go with me to Dallas and you will be able to see your homeboy there next week."

The tall man said, "Okay, I am going to go with you to Dallas. I want to see and talk to my homeboy. I haven't seen Christopher since 1944, the year he got out of the army, four years ago."

After the two men left the café, Big Junior smiled to himself. He had finally gotten the lucky break that he had been hoping for. He thought to himself, "So, 'Pretty Boy' Marvin's real name is Christopher Stephens and these two guys that just left know him. I'll bet they are into crime just like he is. I am going to Dallas and find that big, fancy nightclub called the Supreme. Boy, don't I have a surprise waiting for slick, 'Pretty Boy' Marvin!"

Big Junior finished his lunch, and then he left immediately for Dallas, Texas. He arrived in Dallas that evening and soon found the big, fancy Supreme Nightclub. He then got himself a room in a hotel overlooking the Supreme Nightclub. From his window in the room, he had an excellent view of the Supreme Nightclub and could see anyone who entered it. The next day, Sunday, Big Junior began his watch for "Pretty Boy" Marvin to appear. He observed the Supreme Nightclub for six days, Sunday morning through Saturday morning, but "Pretty Boy" Marvin never appeared. It was late Saturday evening and Big Junior had become restless when he finally saw a shiny, black 1948 Ford car pull up to the Supreme Nightclub and park on the street. Within a few minutes, a tall, dark, handsome, sharply dressed man stepped out of the car and with him was a tall, sexy lady. Big Junior recognized the man as "Pretty Boy"

Marvin himself.

As soon as "Pretty Boy" Marvin and his lady went inside the nightclub, Big Junior went downstairs to the hotel lobby and called the Dallas police. He told them about the criminal Marvin McKinley, how he had manipulated the town of Happyville, Oklahoma out of $25,000, and that he was inside the Supreme Nightclub. Within ten minutes, five Dallas policemen were on the scene. Big Junior walked over to the nightclub with the policemen to point out Marvin McKinley. Once inside the nightclub, Big Junior pointed him out to the policemen. When they saw Marvin McKinley, they recognized him as a criminal they had been looking for. They quickly surrounded him and put him in handcuffs.

When "Pretty Boy" Marvin saw Big Junior standing in front of him as he was being led to the police car, he had a sad and disbelieving look on his face. He couldn't believe that Big Junior, the country bumpkin, had been smart enough to track him down, and cause him to be arrested.

From a newspaper article that appeared in the Dallas newspaper the next day, Big Junior learned some interesting things about "Pretty Boy" Marvin. His real name was Christopher Stephens but he used the false names Marvin McKinley and Carlos Hodges. He had been born in Tulsa and raised in Oklahoma City and Dallas. He had graduated from high school and college in Texas. He had entered the U.S. Army in 1940; he had been a good soldier, seeing action in World War II in Europe, North Africa, and the Far East. However, he had been kicked out of the army in 1944 for insubordination. He had lied to Carmen about what he had done when he left the army. He hadn't worked or taken business courses in Baltimore, Maryland, instead during that period he had been involved in crime. Since being kicked out of the army, he had operated as a con man in Oklahoma, Texas, and Louisiana. His specialty was manipulating wealthy women. With his charm, he could make highly intelligent women do stupid things by manipulating their emotions. His first crime had occurred in Houston, Texas in 1944. There he had captured a wealthy schoolteacher's heart with his charm and good looks, and had manipulated her out of thousands of dollars. Before his capture, he had been wanted by the police for thievery but had managed to elude them by using false names and other clever tricks. Now that he was caught, his crimes would land him in prison for a long time. Also he had spent the $25,000 he had stolen from the people of Happyfield.

Meanwhile, when Big Junior returned to Happyville, he was very happy and excited. He told Rev. Cotton the whole story about how he had tracked "Pretty Boy" Marvin to Dallas, Texas and had pointed him out to the police, and they had arrested him. News of Marvin McKinley's arrest spread quickly in Happyville. The people were glad to see him behind bars for what he had done to them. Rev. Joseph Cotton spoke for everyone in town when he said, "I'm glad Marvin McKinley has been caught and arrested for stealing our money and others' money also. Although none of the money has been recovered, we are still a blessed and a rich people here in Happyville, because we have something more valuable than silver and gold, and it is called trust."

Big Junior was treated like a hero by the people of Happyville for his determined effort in tracking "Pretty Boy" Marvin down and pointing him out to the police so he could be arrested. He was given a certificate, a monetary award, and numerous standing ovations wherever he spoke in town by the people of Happyville.

In early November Big Junior decided to try to court Carmen Stokes again, who he was secretly in love with. He asked her could he take her out to dinner but as always she rejected him in a nice way. She said, "Big Junior, I am still trying to get over my painful relationship with Marvin McKinley. However, when I get over it I will let you know."

Carmen's sly rejection hurt Big Junior but he tried not to let it get him down. He thought to himself, "I hope one day she will realize how much I love her and how good a man I am."

When Carmen's Aunt Sarah heard through the grapevine that Carmen had rejected Big Junior again, she got kind of upset. She said to her son, "Sonny, I'm going to have to talk to that Carmen. She doesn't know a good man when she sees one. 'Big Junior' Coleman has some good qualities, but she just can't see them."

The next day, Aunt Sarah went over to Carmen's house to visit her and to tell her what was on her mind. She said to Carmen, "Girl, I came over here to tell you some truthful things about yourself. I'm going to tell you the truth and if you never speak to me again, that is all right. I just have to tell you some truthful things about yourself."

Carmen replied, "Aunt Sarah, go ahead and tell me what you think about me. I know it will probably hurt but I won't get mad at you."

Aunt Sarah said, "I heard through the grapevine the other day that you have again rejected Big Junior's offer to take you out."

Carmen replied, "Aunt Sarah, you heard it right. I sure did reject Big Junior's offer to take me out to dinner. But I did it in a nice way. You see, he just isn't the man for me. Big Junior is not an ugly man, but he just does not have himself together. I don't like the way he dresses, and I don't like his plain style. He wears those out of style suits that are too small for him, and he wears that old -fashioned haircut. I like for my man to be in style and looking good when he goes out with me. I also like for my man to have a little flash and flair."

Aunt Sarah said, "Girl, let me tell you something. The men with all that flash and flair that you have courted didn't want you. All they wanted was what they could get from you. They used you. Your former husband, Ronald Stokes, used you. He was handsome and full of flair but he was 'no good.' That's the reason why you all's marriage eventually deteriorated to the point that you had to divorce. And 'Pretty Boy' Marvin was slicker than slick. He really used you and then broke your heart. My point is, you need to begin judging the book by its content rather than by its cover. You need to wake up and judge men more by what is on the inside of them than what is on the outside of them. The old saying says 'All that looks like gold isn't gold.' What I've been trying to tell you is this: Big Junior may not be very attractive from the outside, but he has some outstanding qualities on the inside. And the most important thing is, he wants you. It isn't worth a can of beans if the person you want doesn't want you. Get someone who wants you. Big Junior would give anything to date you. Go out with him at least one time. Then if you don't like him, you just don't like him."

The naked truth that Aunt Sarah told Carmen had her in tears. She had never been told the truth about herself like that before. After wiping her eyes, she said, "Aunt Sarah, everything you have said about me is the truth. But it hurts so much! I'll go out with Big Junior if he asks me to. However, if I see the relationship isn't going anywhere, I'm going to give it up."

Aunt Sarah said, "Yes, Carmen, I understand what you are saying, and I am not trying to run your life. I'm just trying to give you some knowledge that I have gained from experience. I have already walked the road that you still have to travel."

Aunt Sarah had talked to Carmen, now she wanted to have a few words with "Big Junior" Coleman. She went to his store and told him she had something to tell him when he got off work.

That evening Big Junior stopped by Aunt Sarah's house. When he walked inside, he greeted her warmly and sat down in a chair. She said to him, "Big Junior, I'm not trying to meddle in your business, but I heard through the grapevine that my niece, Carmen, has rejected your offer to take her out to dinner again."

Big Junior replied, "Mrs. Sarah, she sure has. I guess she just doesn't like me."

Aunt Sarah said, "Big Junior, Carmen is my niece, but she hasn't always been a good selector of men. She generally selects a man who looks good to her instead of a man who would be good for her. She likes her man to be a good dresser and to give her nice compliments."

Big Junior replied, "Mrs. Sarah, I understand what you are saying."

Aunt Sarah said, "Big Junior, I like you and I am trying to help you. So, don't take what I am about to say personally. Big Junior, you need to dress better. Buy yourself some clothes that are in style. Quit wearing those suits that have high-water pants and coats with sleeves halfway up your arms. Buy some suits that fit your body properly. Quit letting Mr. T.J. cut your hair. Start wearing the haircut that is in style. And most of all, quit wearing shoes with mud on them. Start wearing shoes that have been shined. Also give women compliments, and tell them how good they look."

Aunt Sarah's frank criticism had Big Junior shaking and mumbling to himself. No one had ever been that frank with him before in a constructive way. He said to her, "Mrs. Sarah, your constructive criticism has cut through me like a sharp knife cuts through butter. But what you said is the truth and it hurts. I'm going to dress better and get myself together."

About a week after his talk with Aunt Sarah, Big Junior asked Carmen again would she go out to dinner with him. He was very surprised when she told him yes. But he was very happy that she had said yes. Big Junior and Carmen agreed to have dinner at Rose's Restaurant that Friday evening.

When Big Junior picked up Carmen in his car that Friday evening for dinner, she couldn't believe how good he looked. He wore a stylish brown suit that fitted his muscular body perfectly, a pair of spit-polished brown shoes, a pretty brown hat, and a gold watch. His haircut also looked nice and was in style. Carmen was so outdone that she asked, "Big Junior, is this really you?"

Big Junior answered with a chuckle, "Yes, Carmen, this is me."

Carmen and Big Junior had a very enjoyable Friday evening together. Their dinner was delicious at Rose's Restaurant. They even went to the movies after they finished dinner. When Big Junior drove Carmen home, he told her how much he had enjoyed the evening with her. He said, "Carmen, this date with you was the most enjoyable date I have ever had. And you are the prettiest woman that I have ever dated. I hope you will go out with me again."

Carmen replied, "Big Junior, thanks for the compliments. I have enjoyed myself with you, too. Of course, I will go out with you again."

Big Junior and Carmen continued to date. During the winter of 1948-49 they enjoyed going to dances and basketball games together. Big Junior also took Carmen hunting, something that she hadn't done before. When spring arrived Big Junior and Carmen continued to enjoy going out together. During the summer they especially enjoyed their time together. They went fishing, horseback riding, and canoeing. They turned heads with their hand-in-hand walks around town. By fall Carmen was falling in love with Big Junior who was already madly in love with her.

One day in October Aunt Sarah stopped by Carmen's house for a visit. She asked Carmen, "Girl, how is your relationship with Big Junior going?"

Carmen answered, "Aunt Sarah, I am falling in love with Earnest 'Big Junior' Coleman. Can you believe that?"

Aunt Sarah said, "What? You are falling in love with 'Big Junior' Coleman? That is wonderful. I told you last year that if you dated him you would get to like him."

Carmen replied, "Yes, Aunt Sarah, I am falling in love with Big Junior. He is not as charming and as flashy as the other guys that I have courted, but he has some qualities that I really admire. He is strong and gentle. I like for him to hold me in his arms. I feel so secure when I am in his arms. He is also ambitious, determined, intelligent, caring, and honest. He is the real thing and not a phony. When he tells me he loves me, I know he means it. I admire him a lot."

Aunt Sarah said, "Girl, I didn't know that you admired Big Junior that much."

Carmen said, "Yes, Aunt Sarah, I sure do. He has qualities that you won't see until you get to know him."

Big Junior and Carmen continued their romance. As the months passed, they grew closer together. By the spring of 1950 Carmen was in love with Big Junior and he was so very, very much in love with her. In June Big Junior asked Carmen to marry him and she said yes. Carmen's decision made Big Junior very happy. The wedding date was set for the Friday after Thanksgiving Day.

On the wedding day, a huge crowd gathered inside Happyville's A.M.E. Church to see Earnest "Big Junior" Coleman and Carmen Stokes get married. Rev. Joseph Cotton performed the wedding ceremony. Big Junior was so happy to have Carmen as his wife. It was a dream come true. Also many people in town were happy to see them get married, especially Aunt Sarah.

About two weeks after their wedding, as Big Junior and Carmen drove home from Oklahoma City, Big Junior said, "I am so glad to have you for my wife. I love you so very, very much. Words cannot adequately express how much I love you. I believe we are going to be very successful as a team. We are going to build the clothing factory that 'Pretty Boy' Marvin talked about building but never built. I want to see Happyville, Oklahoma grow into a large town with thriving industries and businesses. I even hope one day we have a college here like in Langston."

Carmen said, "Big Junior, I love you so very much, too. I wouldn't trade you for a thousand Marvin McKinleys. And I mean that. When you tell me you love me, I know you mean it. When you tell me you will never leave me, I believe you. Big Junior, we are going to do big things together as a team. We are going to make sure that the clothing factory is built here in Happyville so it can create jobs. We are also going to work together to make Happyville, Oklahoma a better place to live and to raise a family."

ANALYSIS OF STORY

The story "What Is More Valuable Than Silver and Gold?" revolves around the value of trust to the town of Happyville, Oklahoma. Happyville was founded on trust. Because the people of Happyville trusted each other, they could always depend upon each other in times of need and trouble. Trust enabled the town to survive its difficult early beginning in the 1890s. It also enabled the town to survive the Great Depression of the 1930s. In short, trust was the most valuable asset the town had, more valuable than silver and gold.

In 1946 a tall, dark, handsome, sharply dressed stranger named Marvin McKinley rode into the town of Happyville. He was friendly and charming and he soon won the trust of many of the townspeople. He also captured the heart of pretty and wealthy Carmen Stokes with his charm. After he captured Carmen's heart, a love triangle developed among him, Carmen, and Big Junior, a man who also wanted Carmen's love. Eventually a furious fight erupted between "Pretty Boy" Marvin and Big Junior over Carmen. Big Junior was blamed for starting the fight, which damaged his credibility among the people of Happyville. They thought he talked negative about "Pretty Boy" Marvin because he was jealous of his successful romance with Carmen. On the other hand, the fight enhanced "Pretty Boy" Marvin's credibility among the people of Happyville, and enabled him to win the trust of the few people in town that had been skeptical of him. The few skeptics now believed he was a nice guy and Big Junior had started the fight with him and was suspicious of him out of jealousy. With all the people in town trusting him except Big Junior, "Pretty Boy" Marvin was able to con them out of $25,000 to pay a construction company to build a clothing factory in Happyville. Once "Pretty Boy" Marvin got the money in his hands, he skipped town and never returned. His manipulative scheme destroyed the trust among the people of Happyville, causing them to be suspicious and selfish with each other. However, thanks to the great effort of "Little Johnny" Allbright in bringing the people together again, trust was eventually restored in Happyville.

This story teaches the importance of trust, which is more valuable than silver and gold. Without trust, it is very difficult to maintain group unity. For example, successful marriages, organizations, and even nations have fallen apart because of a lack of trust. There have been marriages, organizations, and nations that had plenty of silver and gold but fell apart because of dishonesty and corruption.

Dishonesty breeds distrust and suspicion. When a partner cheats in a marriage, that causes distrust. When an official steals from his organization, that causes distrust. When a leader lies to the people in his nation, that causes distrust. In short, dishonesty breeds distrust and suspicion, which are destroyers of trust.

Distrust also causes selfishness. Where there is a lack of trust, people will be reluctant to share with or help others because they will be afraid their kindness maybe taken advantage of.

The point here is trust is very valuable. It is more valuable than silver and gold. It is critical to maintaining group unity. It also encourages a safe environment where people feel unafraid to practice the system of sharing and caring.

CONCLUSION

These four stories have dealt with people overcoming adversity and solving problems through their intelligence, strength, humor, and determination.

It is the author's hope that these stories can serve as a source of strength, inspiration, knowledge, and understanding to the reader.

These stories are about the black experience—a story of black people's struggle to overcome hard times and adversity in America from slavery to the present.

Finally, black people have been telling stories for a long, long time and these stories are a continuation of that tradition.

NOTES ON INTRODUCTION

1. J.A. Rogers, *World's Great Men of Color, Vol. I,* Introduction by John Henrik Clarke, Macmillan Publishing Co., Inc., New York, 1972, revised edition, p. 67.
2. Ibid., p. 79.
3. Ibid., p. 75.
4. Ibid., p. 75.

ABOUT THE AUTHOR

Robert L. Bradley was born in Memphis, Tennessee. He is employed as a cartographer (mapmaker). He has been studying the history of black people since the fourth grade. He also enjoys writing short stories and poetry. He holds a B.A. degree in history from Tennessee State University of Nashville, Tennessee and a M.S. degree in geography from the University of Memphis (formerly Memphis State University).

STORIES ABOUT THE
BLACK
EXPERIENCE

THEY ALL CAME TOGETHER TO UPLIFT THE COMMUNITY

VOLUME TWO

To order a copy of this book, write to:

Robert L. Bradley
P.O. Box 25768
St. Louis, MO 63136